# Settlers Valley

# Settlers Valley

JERRY APPS

THE UNIVERSITY OF WISCONSIN PRESS

The University of Wisconsin Press
728 State Street, Suite 443
Madison, Wisconsin 53706
uwpress.wisc.edu

Gray's Inn House, 127 Clerkenwell Road
London ECIR 5DB, United Kingdom
eurospanbookstore.com

Printed in the United States of America
This book may be available in a digital edition.

Library of Congress Cataloging-in-Publication Data

Names: Jerold W., 1934- author.
Title: Settlers Valley / Jerry Apps.
Description: Madison, Wisconsin :
The University of Wisconsin Press, [2021]
Identifiers: LCCN 2020036108 | ISBN 9780299332143 (paperback)
Subjects: LCGFT: Fiction. | Novels.
Classification: LCC PS3601.P67 S48 2021 | DDC 813/.54—dc23
LC record available at https://lccn.loc.gov/2020036108

*To all disabled veterans*

# Settlers Valley

# I

The big German shepherd got up from his rug behind the kitchen woodstove and padded to the bedroom. There he found C.J. Anderson, still asleep. The big dog stopped by the bed, looking at his master, listening to his quiet breathing, and wagging his tail. He stepped forward, stuck out his tongue, and licked C.J. on the face.

C.J.'s eyes snapped open.

"Lucky, it's you," he said, patting the big dog on the head.

C.J. got out of bed, found his prosthetic leg, attached it, and pulled on a red-checked flannel shirt and a worn pair of blue jeans. He walked out to the kitchen with Lucky at his side, ready to support his master if necessary. C.J. was twenty-eight, a big man of about six foot three with a ruddy complexion. Since moving to Ames County two years ago, he had worn a full black beard. He opened a kitchen cupboard and saw the bottle of Jack Daniels. Oh, how he once depended on his bottled friend to get him through the day. But the bottle had not been touched since he arrived in Settlers Valley. Retrieving the can of coffee, he dumped some in the coffee pot and plugged it in.

He crumpled up some old newspapers, pushed them into the cookstove, added a few sticks of kindling wood, and touched a match to paper. He had learned how to cook on this relic of a stove from his grandfather Oscar Anderson, who lived just a half mile down the road from C.J.'s little log cabin in the woods, as his grandfather called it. He opened the kitchen door to let Lucky outside and filled the shepherd's dish with dog food.

C.J. had built this log cabin with the help of several of his veteran friends. It was one story with a combined living room and dining room area, two bedrooms—one C.J. used as his office but could also serve as a guest room—and a bathroom. It had a covered porch on the front and an open deck on the back. C.J. prided himself on generating his own energy with both a wind turbine and solar panels.

He poured a cup of coffee and stepped outside to the porch, where Lucky waited. He sat on his Aldo Leopold bench. The simple, angular bench named after the famed conservationist had been one of C.J.'s first carpentry projects. Not only was it comfortable, but when he sat on it, it reminded him of Leopold's writings and how they had influenced him to take up his grandfather's gift of this land.

C.J. had grown up in Madison, where his father had been a professor at the University of Wisconsin. His parents had died in a car accident when he was on his last tour in Afghanistan. C.J. thought the only thing about that tragedy that could be considered a blessing was that they hadn't had to see him suffer when he was hit by a roadside bomb and ended up losing his right leg below the knee.

C.J. had grown up a city boy, but he spent his summers working on his grandfather's farm in Ames County. Now he lived on a back corner of that farm. When C.J. had returned home from Afghanistan—missing a leg, mourning his parents, an alcoholic, and uncertain what to do with his life—he had had many lengthy discussions with his grandfather about how to pick up the pieces. Oscar Anderson had given him five acres of land.

C.J. had kept in contact with several of his fellow veterans he had gotten to know while at Walter Reed Hospital in Maryland. His reports about his life as a small-scale farmer in central Wisconsin had convinced some of them to join him in Settlers Valley. Oscar Anderson had talked with several of his farmer neighbors in Settlers Valley, encouraging them to rent small acreages of land to these veterans, with rent-to-buy agreements. All of the landowners agreed. Now, just two years later, twenty veterans and their families were renting small acreages in Settlers Valley. Most of the vets were in their late twenties or early thirties. Some, like C.J., had lost limbs or had some other combat-related disability; all had some degree of post-traumatic stress disorder (PTSD).

Other than C.J., none of the vets had farming experience. They all leaned heavily on Oscar Anderson and another local retired farmer, Fred Russo, who together served as informal consultants to the group and offered the use of their equipment as well. With the help of these old-time farmers, the veterans and their families had already established an impressive array of small farming operations. Most grew vegetables, including lettuce, sweet corn, radishes, beets, green beans, yellow beans, kale, carrots, and potatoes. One raised pasture-fed hogs, and another had free-range chickens and maintained several bee-hives in a small aviary. Raising sheep for wool became the passion of one vet. Another grew hops and barley to supply the recently opened Link Lake Brewery. One disabled vet and his wife raised milking goats. They worked out an arrangement with the Link Lake Cheese Factory to make cheese, which they labeled "Old Settlers Goat Cheese." His wife made goat milk candles and goat milk soaps that had begun to sell well.

The veterans called themselves the Back to the Land Veterans. They held a well-attended farmers' market in Link Lake every Saturday in summer. Recently they had formed the Back to the Land Grocery Cooperative, which operated out of an old building on Main Street in Link Lake. There they sold homegrown vegetables, fruits and meats, homemade jellies and jams, home-knitted sweaters from the vet who raised sheep, Old Settlers Goat Cheese, and goat milk candles. They maintained a small office in the back of the store staffed by the store manager—another veteran—and volunteers.

With Lucky by his side, C.J. looked to the east and watched the sunrise. Oh, how he enjoyed seeing the sun as it slowly climbed over the trees, sending long shadows down Settlers Valley, where Settlers Creek meandered like a drunken sailor. He could hear the water bouncing off rocks and moving over the gravel bottom. For C.J. there were few things more relaxing, more soothing, to his troubled psyche than the sound of flowing water. Save for the gurgling of the stream, and the occasional raucous cry of a crow in the distance, the morning was quiet. C.J. savored the quiet, but he also enjoyed the sounds of nature, which helped him heal.

Doctors at Walter Reed told him that he was suffering from PTSD and had lots of healing to do, both mentally and physically. After several months of counseling and physical rehabilitation, he was discharged, but he was far from healed.

Returning inside, C.J. sat down and began writing in his journal, something a doctor at the hospital suggested he regularly do. He wrote:

Looks like a beautiful April day in Ames County. I mostly slept through the night, no nightmares for a change. No recalling of that fateful day in Afghanistan when our truck drove over an IED and exploded, killing six of my friends and leaving me with a missing leg. But will it last? What about tonight? I remember as a kid staying with Grandpa Anderson, sitting with him in the dark and looking at the stars flickering so many thousands of miles away. How I enjoyed those dark nights. But not now. The night is too often filled with dreams I don't want to dream, and memories I don't want to remember. The night is my enemy. The night is a monster. It reminds me that life is a bitch, and it doesn't get better, especially at night. The night is filled with demons, those damnable demons. Always there. Jumping out from behind trees. Calling from the moon. Calling my name. Demons. Sometimes they come in the daytime too. Especially during cloudy days. Always calling my name. How do these damn demons know my name? Oh, God, how do I get rid of them? Will I ever get rid of them? Living this life is hell.

Closing his journal, he poured a second cup of coffee and sat down by the cookstove and rubbed his eyes with his hand. He thought about the letter he had sent off to the *Ames County Argus* and wondered what kind of reaction he would get. Most people living in Link Lake were pleased with the recognition that C.J. had gotten nationally for his approach to helping disabled veterans heal and get on with their lives while working the soil. But not everyone was so inclined.

Two groups in the area were especially critical of what C.J. and his small group of veterans were doing. The ultraconservative Eagle Party was slowly gaining strength in Ames County. They had accused the Back to the Land Veterans of being socialists and going against what they called the American Way, which applauded the accumulation of wealth and little more. The other disapproving group, led by the Reverend Jacob John Jacob, pastor of the Church of the Holy Redeemed, felt that anyone whose spiritual beliefs were not in tune with theirs was headed straight to hell, with no stopping along the way. There was overlap between the two groups as Eagle Party members made up a substantial proportion of the Church of the Holy Redeemed's membership.

Most of the veterans and their families avoided Pastor Jacob's church and instead attended the Link Lake People's Church, founded recently by Pastor Vicki Emerson, a fellow disabled veteran who had served as a military chaplain for several years. The church, nondenominational, was open to everyone who wanted to attend but was especially attuned to the needs of the disabled veterans in the area. Pastor Vicki, a trained counselor, also made house calls in the community.

C.J. thought about these things as he set to work at his kitchen table planting tomato, cabbage, and broccoli seeds into little fiber containers, where they would germinate. He placed the containers on a shelf in front of one of the south-facing cabin windows. When the plants had grown to a couple of inches or so, he would transplant them into larger pots and then wait until the weather was right for transplanting them in his two-acre market garden. Lucky watched every move he made but stayed out of the way as C.J. worked.

There was a quiet knock on the door.

"Who is it?" asked C.J.

Lucky got up and trotted toward the door. C.J. had few visitors, and he liked it that way.

"It's Pastor Vicki."

C.J. hobbled toward the door and opened it, Lucky standing by his side.

"Come on in. A little chilly out there this morning," he said.

"Thank you," said the pastor. She was about five foot two, with long, black hair tied in a braid in back, and a faint scar above her right eye. "How are you doing today?" she asked. "Did you hear we've started planning for the spring rhubarb festival?" She petted Lucky as she talked. She knew how important a dog could be for someone recovering from a devastating health challenge.

"My rhubarb's looking pretty good," C.J. replied.

"You did know the festival is featuring rhubarb pie and rhubarb wine this year?" asked the pastor. "You should enter some wine."

"I'll have to think about it—I've been known to make some decent rhubarb wine."

"Join the competition, C.J." the pastor said, smiling.

"I just might do that," said C.J. "I just might."

# 2

*Ames County Argus*
### Pipeline Has Eye on Central Wisconsin

The Al-Mid Pipeline Company, which has offices in Edmonton, Alberta, and Minneapolis, is planning to build a new pipeline to stretch from the oil fields of Alberta to a refinery in Illinois, said a spokesman for the company. A definite route has not been selected for the 30 inch pipeline designed to transport more than 400,000 barrels of crude oil a day. Company officials are exploring several possible choices for the pipeline in Wisconsin, but no further details were offered. One of the possible routes includes threading through central Wisconsin.

On a sunny, bright Wednesday morning in mid-April, Oscar Anderson and Fred Russo took their usual seats in the Eat Well Café on Main Street in Link Lake. It was seven thirty. The two farmers, both in their eighties, had sat in these same chairs at this same table, near this same window, for twenty years. Oscar and Fred had grown up together, attended a one-room country school together, and then farmed next to each other until they both held auctions selling off their cattle. That same year they had decided that with no cows to milk, and therefore no reason to get up at five thirty every morning, on Wednesdays they would sit down together, drink a little coffee, eat a restaurant-prepared breakfast, and talk about anything, everything, and often nothing. For a while they met every morning but now met once a week.

Oscar and Fred didn't agree on everything. Oscar was the progressive one: the first in the neighborhood to try hybrid seed corn, to buy a tractor with a cab on it, to switch from shipping milk in ten-gallon milk cans to using a bulk tank holding enough milk that the milkman only had to stop by his farm every other day.

Fred liked to keep things as they were. He farmed with horses long after everyone in their neighborhood had switched to tractors and put their horses out to graze. He never increased the size of his dairy herd beyond twenty or so milk cows. He refused to plant new hybrid varieties of corn and grains.

They also agreed on several things, such as the importance of family—both had lost their wives several years earlier; both had grown children who had moved away but regularly visited. They agreed on the importance of neighbors working together helping and supporting one another, doing a neighbor's work when there was an injury or illness in the family, and sharing birthday parties and anniversaries.

But it was their love for the land that knitted the men together like brothers. Fred's farm was 160 acres, the same size it was when it was homesteaded back in 1866. Oscar had inherited his farm from his father; at the time it was 160 acres as well, the standard size for many farms in Wisconsin. He had added more land as the years had passed and now owned 320 acres, with about 100 acres of it wooded.

Oscar and Fred both drove their own pickup trucks to town. Fred owned an old green Ford F-150; Oscar had a shiny black three-year-old Toyota Tacoma. Another of their disagreements.

"Never drive one of them foreign pickups," Fred often said.

With their coffee cups filled and their breakfasts ordered, Fred asked, "So what's new with you, Oscar? Got any new aches and pains?"

"None," said Oscar, grumpily.

Fred held up his hand. "Jeez, you're a bit testy this morning. You fall out of bed or something?"

"I did not fall out of bed," said Oscar after taking a big drink of coffee.

"You goin' to the school forest celebration?" asked Fred.

"Yes, I am," said Oscar. "Do you remember the spring seventy years ago when we helped plant the first trees in the school forest? Somebody had just given the school some hundred acres of sandy, hilly land in northern Ames County."

"Yup, remember it well," said Fred. "We planted about five thousand trees that spring, all Norway pine and all by hand. Kind of fun, it was. A few days away from school and a chance to be outdoors. Every one of the high school seniors helped plant. Boys and girls. Bunch of younger kids too."

The waitress put a stack of pancakes in front of each of the old friends, and for a while the only sound in the little restaurant was that of quiet conversation going on as other customers worked on their eggs, slices of bacon with American fries, or giant cinnamon buns with white frosting dripping off the sides. Several customers ordered stacks of pancakes, just like those in front of Oscar and Fred. The smell of freshly brewed coffee and bacon frying hung politely in the air, not too much, just enough to add to the homey atmosphere the Eat Well Café was noted for.

In between bites of pancakes, Fred broke the silence.

"How are things with that grandson of yours, C.J.? He still feelin' like a 'local hero with a big idea,' like they called him in that piece in *Reader's Digest* last winter?"

"Yup, that's what they said, but C.J. wasn't too pleased," Oscar replied. "When the *Reader's Digest* people tried to call him for an interview, he wouldn't talk with them. Said what he had done in Afghanistan was best forgotten, and the men and women who died fighting there were the real heroes, not him. Said that his idea for curin' some of the hurt from the war by returnin' to the land was the business of the veterans living in Settlers Valley—not somethin' the world should know about. Somehow the *Reader's Digest* folks heard that I was his grandfather, so they called me up."

"Was C.J. ticked off with you for talkin' with them?" asked Fred.

"I suppose a little. C.J.'s a pretty private guy these days—probably because of his injuries. Besides having lost most of his right leg, he's got a tough case of PTSD."

"PT—what is it again?"

"Post-traumatic stress disorder. Lots of returnin' vets have it. C.J. doesn't want folks to know he has it. He mostly wants to be left alone and only wants to talk to other vets. He's told me a little about what his life is like these days—not being able to sleep, headaches, feelings of worthlessness, guilt. If C.J. has told me once, he's told me a hundred times that he doesn't know why he's alive when so many of his buddies were killed."

"Sounds awful," said Fred, taking another drink of coffee.

"It is awful," Oscar agreed. "I'm hopin' C.J. will recover. Losin' his folks in a car accident surely didn't help. When C.J. came back from the war, he didn't know what to do next. When I offered those five acres to him, I didn't tell him that land has its own way of healin' people. If I had he probably would have turned me down. I also didn't share the history of our valley with him. I will do it sometime. You know it, don't you, Fred? You know the history of our valley?"

"Well, I know that Rolf Russo homesteaded my farm in 1866, right after the Civil War. I know he fought in the war. That much I know," said Fred.

"When I gave the land to C.J., I went to the library and did a little diggin'. I didn't know much about our valley, and I didn't know who named it Settlers Valley," said Oscar.

"So what'd you find out?" asked Fred.

"Hold your horses. Give me a second to get it all straight in my head," said Oscar.

"I'm not sure you ever had anything straight in your head." Fred chuckled.

Oscar ignored his friend's comment and began. "The story starts back in 1866, when your ancestor, one Rolf Russo, and my ancestor, one Nels Anderson, both Civil War vets, heard about the 1862 Homestead Act. The law said folks like them could settle on 160 acres of federally owned land, and if they made a go of it, meanin' they put up some buildings and broke some land, the property would be theirs free and clear in five years. Kind of like gettin' land for free, it was." Oscar paused to take another sip of coffee.

"Well, I'm guessin' these two guys were suffering some of the same of what C.J. and his fellow disabled vets are sufferin' today, way back in 1866," he continued. "Of course, I'm guessin' that nobody knew anything about PTSD then. They probably didn't call it 'shell shock' then either—that's what they called it when I was in the army back during the Korean War."

"Well, I'll be," said Fred.

"There's more. These two guys took up farmin', and they invited several other Civil War vets to come here and farm as well—and one day, when they were all together, puttin' up one of their barns, they got to talkin' about what to name the valley where we now live. They came up with Settlers Valley, and the name stuck."

"Well, that's pretty darn interestin', Oscar. Pretty darn interestin'," Fred said as he chased the last piece of pancake around his plate. "Kind of interestin' that your grandson and some of his fellow soldiers are doin' the same thing today," said Fred. "The land is a great teacher, but it can also be a healer."

"Fred, you know I couldn't agree more," Oscar said. "It's kind of like the way you and I have been teachin' these new young farmers about rotatin' crops. A lot of these small acreages they're rentin' were nearly ruined by previous owners growing the same thing year after year. And you and I know some of those old-timers used massive amounts of fertilizer and pesticides, which didn't do the soil any favors, either. Good thing we've been showin' them how to build back the health of their fields. As the land helps heal these veterans, the veterans are healin' the land."

"You think C.J. is gettin' better?" Fred asked.

"Yeah, I do," said Oscar, putting down his cup. "It's been a couple years. I know he's gone through a personal hell. Since the *Reader's Digest* story, he's been gettin' calls and emails from people all over the country, mostly veterans, but also burned-out young executives lookin' for a different way of life. More of these folks are considerin' moving here to Link Lake to be part of his group, the Back to the Land Veterans."

"So isn't that what he wants? More folks agreein' with him and wantin' to be a part of what he started, wantin' to return to the land?"

"Well, yes and no. As you know, it was C.J. and a handful of his fellow Afghanistan vets who all agreed to try what he is tryin'. They all have similar backgrounds, similar interests."

"So, what's the problem?" asked Fred.

"C.J. wants people to have the same love for the land that he has. But he wants a lot more. He doesn't want a bunch of folks who think they want to return to the land and don't have a clue as to why, other than somethin' they've read in a "love the land" publication. He wants people comin' who know how to work, know how to get their hands dirty, know how to get up in the mornin' and work all day. And do it again the next day, and the day after that."

"Sounds like how we farmed." Fred chuckled.

"Say, Fred, did you see the piece about an oil pipeline comin' to Wisconsin?" Oscar asked, changing the subject.

"I did. Wonder what that's about. I sure can't imagine any pipeline wantin' to build here. Too many hills," said Fred. "Gotta go pretty soon. You got one of those thoughts for the day—somethin' your pa always said?"

"How about this?" said Oscar. "If you're doin' nothin', how do you know when you're finished?"

"You wouldn't be referrin' to yourself, now would you, Oscar?" Fred laughed as he got up, put on his International Harvester cap, and headed for the door.

# 3

Margaret Werch was a city girl born and raised in Chicago. She was of medium height, with long blonde hair that she usually wore in a ponytail and big blue eyes that lit up her face when she talked. Maggie, as she liked to be called, had a connection to Link Lake, and she remembered it fondly. She, her parents, and her brother had spent two weeks every summer vacationing in a little cottage on Silver Lake, just east of the Village of Link Lake. Maggie remembered swimming in the clear blue waters of Silver Lake, fishing with her dad, and watching the sunset with her family while listening to the sounds of the evening, bullfrog choruses, and an owl calling in the woods to the north.

When Maggie graduated from high school, she enlisted in the army. After two tours in Afghanistan and a total of ten years in the service, she returned home. Now, even with the opportunity to have the government pay for her college education, at age twenty-eight, she didn't think college was for her. Her former boyfriend, who had said he would always be there for her, had married another girl.

By her first Christmas back in Chicago, she was near homeless. She worked at a fast food place in Chicago; her meager income barely paid her rent. She was too proud to move home. She suffered by herself, well aware that she probably had PTSD. She had even contemplated taking her own life. Quite by chance, she read in *Reader's Digest* about C.J. Anderson's "back to the land" movement in Wisconsin. She had kept a copy of the magazine and found it two years later when she was searching through the clutter in the bottom of her clothes closet. *Maybe this is something I should do,* she had thought after she read the article again. *I'm going nowhere with my life. But killing myself is not the answer.*

She made the decision to move to Link Lake and take up farming shortly after the new year. She contacted the Back to the Land Veterans office, and someone there had put her in touch with a retired farmer in the Settlers Valley community willing to rent Maggie five acres of land with a right to purchase. In early March, she moved into the old abandoned farmhouse on the property. Although the old wooden frame house had electricity, there was no electric stove in the kitchen. All the cooking had been done on a wood-burning cookstove. The stove appeared a bit rusty but otherwise seemed to be in working order. Maggie had never considered herself much of a cook, but with no fast food or other restaurants close by, she would have to learn.

Even after a month of living on the farm, Maggie still sometimes struggled to start the old stove. She remembered the first time she had tried to cook, when she had quickly discovered that she didn't even know how to turn on the stove, suddenly realizing that a wood-burning stove had no "on" button. At that moment, feelings of desperation and worthlessness had once more engulfed her. She had sat down on an old wooden chair and began crying, pulling up the collar of her heavy wool sweater. At least there had been no one around to ask why she was sobbing. Not more than five minutes had passed before she had heard something and quickly glanced out the window. A red pickup truck had pulled up alongside her ancient Toyota, and she had seen a tall, fit-looking man with a black beard walking toward the house. She had noticed that he walked with a limp. He had stopped at the kitchen door and knocked.

Maggie had quickly dried her eyes, pushed a tangle of hair from her face, and opened the door. The tall man had smiled. "I'm C.J. Anderson," he had said. "May I come in?"

"Yes, yes, come in," she had said, quickly recognizing the name.

"It's a bit chilly in here," C.J had said.

"It is. But I can't figure out how to turn on this old stove."

C.J. had laughed. "Well there is no 'turning on' with these old wood burners. What you've got to do is start a fire in it."

"How do I do that?" Maggie had asked. She had liked the sound of C.J.'s voice, confident, self-assured, friendly.

"I'll show you," C.J. had said, glancing toward the wood box. It still had wood in it, and a small pile of newspapers stacked near it. He had also spotted a matchbox holder above the wood box.

C.J. had lifted a lid on the stove, crumpled up a few pieces of newspaper, and stuffed them into the stove. Then he had taken a couple of small sticks of pine wood, placed them on top of the crumpled paper, struck a match, and held the flame to the newspaper. When the flames had begun licking at the wood, he had closed the lid.

"That's all there is to it. I used what my Grandpa Anderson calls kindlin' wood along with the old newspapers. Kindlin' wood catches fire faster than oak wood," C.J. had said as he reached into the wood box for a piece of oak. "Once the fire is going pretty good, you put in a couple pieces of oak wood and you're all set. Before you know it, it'll be as toasty in here as a sunny day in Florida."

"Thank you," Maggie had said. She had detected a slight smoky smell coming from C.J.'s clothing.

"How long were you in the army?" C.J. had asked.

"Ten years. Two tours in Afghanistan, the rest stateside," Maggie had said as she stared at the old woodstove, wondering if it would do what C.J. had said it would.

"What branch?"

"Military police. The last few years on active duty I worked as a criminal investigator."

"One of those," C.J. had said and chuckled. "I can remember a time or two when I was younger and a bit wilder and crossed paths with an MP who showed me the error of my ways."

"Got a lot of memories," Maggie had said. "Mostly bad."

C.J. had caught her tone and quickly changed the subject. "Well, I'm here to welcome you to Settlers Valley and to our Back to the Land Veterans group. If I could be so bold as to ask, what are your plans?"

"Well, to be honest, I'm mostly just running away from something," Maggie had said.

"And that would be?"

"I'm running away from Chicago. I'm broke and I'm nearly homeless. I'm running away from who I am."

C.J. had seen the tears in Maggie's eyes. He had placed a hand on her arm. "You're among friends. The vets here in Settlers Valley have stories not much different from yours."

"I read about what you and the other vets are doing," Maggie had blurted out as tears ran down her face. "I'm no farmer, but I'm . . . I'm willing to learn."

"I'll show you," C.J. had said and embraced Maggie in a big hug. After he had released her, he had handed her a card. "Here's my phone number. Give me a jingle when you want your first farming lesson."

"Thank you," Maggie had said quietly as she wiped tears from her eyes.

"Oh, one more thing. You may have heard of our local church, started by another vet, who was a chaplain. It's called the Link Lake People's Church, and you are most welcome to attend. We meet at 1:00 p.m. on Sunday afternoons."

"I'll try to make it," Maggie had replied, smiling. She couldn't remember the last time she had smiled.

She found herself smiling again as she remembered that first meeting with C.J. and the feelings that had stirred up inside her as she had watched the tall, bearded young man walk toward his pickup and drive away. Maybe it was time to call him up for another farming lesson.

# 4

"My watch says 1:00 p.m. Time to start our little program," said the woman at the microphone in a firm, steady voice. "Thank you for coming. I'm Lucy James, Link Lake School principal. Let's hope the predicted rain holds off for a couple hours. But if it rains, we all know that April showers bring May flowers." Her attempt at a little levity hung helplessly in the cool spring air. Lucy James was tall and thin. She wore her black hair short.

Lucy continued, "Seventy years ago this month we acquired the land for this beautiful school forest and we planted the first trees. We are here today to commemorate that event and dedicate our new shelter. The contractor put the finishing touches on the shelter building just yesterday. Now we can bring students out here in all kinds of weather—it won't matter if it's raining or snowing." She waved her arm toward the new building, which smelled of fresh paint and new concrete.

"We are privileged today," she went on, "to have in our audience two men who helped plant those first trees, Oscar Anderson and Fred Russo, longtime farmers in the Link Lake community. Oscar has a few words to share."

Oscar Anderson, wearing new overalls and a new red plaid shirt, limped up to the podium and took the microphone.

"Can you all hear me way out there in the back forty?" He motioned to the people who were standing in the back of the crowd. "Well," he continued, "who would have thought—certainly not me—that I would be here today to talk about something that I did seventy years ago. Before I go on, I want you to say hello to my old friend and fellow Link Lake classmate, Fred Russo. Fred, hold up your hand."

Fred Russo, also wearing new overalls and a green plaid shirt, held up his arm. People clapped. Russo smiled.

"Are there any others in the audience who helped plant trees here seventy years ago?" asked Oscar. He cupped his left hand over his eyes and stared out over the mass of people attending the event. Three more hands in the back went up.

"As some of you know, I am a lover of trees. I have several acres of them growing on my farm. It was way back in 1946, when I was a little shaver and just old enough to join a 4-H club that my love for trees first began. Forestry was my 4-H project that first year I was a member. One of the requirements of the project was to build a little tree nursery and then plant one-year-old pine trees in it. When the trees were large enough, I planted them around our oak woodlot. They are still there, growing ever taller." Oscar paused for a moment and took a sip of water from the water bottle near the podium.

"Then, when I was a senior at Link Lake, I learned that someone had given the school district this sandy farm, which is only a few miles north of the farm where I grew up and still live to this day. I also learned that the older students at Link Lake would be responsible for planting the first five thousand trees on this new school forest land." Oscar paused again and reached for a little book he had carried with him to the podium.

"This is the school annual for the year that my fellow students and I planted trees. It has several photos of Link Lake students planting trees." Oscar held up a page with the photos that no one except those in the first couple of rows could see.

"I've babbled on long enough. As some of you know, I occasionally write poetry. In fact, in my neighborhood, I am sometimes called the professor of poetry. But today, I am not going to bore you with one of my poems. I want to share a poem that Alfred Joyce Kilmer published back in 1914 about trees. Oscar began reading.

*Trees*
I think that I shall never see
A poem lovely as a tree.
A tree whose hungry mouth is prest
Against the earth's sweet flowing breast;
A tree that looks at God all day,
And lifts her leafy arms to pray;
A tree that may in Summer wear
A nest of robins in her hair;
Upon whose bosom snow has lain;
Who intimately lives with rain.
Poems are made by fools like me,
But only God can make a tree.

"May this school forest continue for many generations to come. Thank you," said Oscar. He took his walking stick and disappeared back into the crowd.

# 5

*Ames County Argus*
## Local Farmer Expands Dairy Herd

John Wilson, who farms west of Link Lake in Settlers Valley, has
plans to increase the size of his dairy herd from 250 milking
cows to 1,000. "In this business of farming, unless you keep
growing you are going out of business," he said in a recent
interview. "With 1,000 milking cows, I will still be running one
of the smaller dairy operations here in Wisconsin. I know of
one that is milking 8,000 cows."

According to a USDA report, the average milk cow in
Wisconsin produces about eight gallons of milk a day. Eight
gallons is about 128 glasses of milk. This means that Wilson's
herd of 1,000 cows would produce about 8,000 gallons of milk a
day. One milk cow will drink between 30 and 50 gallons of water
each day and will eat about 100 pounds of feed each day. Also, a
dairy cow produces on average about 82 pounds of manure a day
per 1,000 pounds of weight. Thus a 1,400-pound Holstein cow
will produce about 115 pounds of manure a day.

A challenge all large dairy operations face is to avoid spreading
the manure where it may contaminate nearby streams or wells.
"We plan on being a good neighbor," Wilson said, "and we are
following all the rules and regulations set down by Wisconsin's

Department of Natural Resources to make sure our manure is handled properly." He added, "Sometimes, our critics don't realize that cow manure is a natural fertilizer providing necessary ingredients to the soil so that record-breaking crop yields can be realized."

The Wednesday after the school forest celebration, Oscar and Fred sat at their regular table at the Eat Well. With their coffee poured and their breakfasts ordered, Fred began the conversation. "So what's new with you, Oscar? Got any new aches and pains?"

"I suppose I do, but what a waste of time it is to sit, slurp coffee, and see which of us can top the other in what new health problem developed during the past week," said Oscar.

"You did a pretty fair job talkin' to that big crowd at the school forest last week," said Fred. "Only one little quibble."

"And that would be?" asked Oscar.

"Well, it was mostly purty good, mostly purty good." Fred hesitated.

"But you said you had a quibble."

"It was just a little one. Just a little quibble."

"Well? You gonna tell me what it was?"

"What would have made your talk one hundred percent perfect instead of only ninety percent perfect was one little thing that you did—more like what you didn't do . . ."

"Jeez, Fred. Spit it out."

"Nobody beyond the first row could see the pictures in our yearbook that you held up. Better if you didn't hold up the pictures at all," said Fred.

"That it? That your quibble?"

"Yup, that's it."

"Thank you for pointing that out to me." Oscar sniffed.

"You're welcome," said Fred, smiling.

The two old men sat quietly for a few moments, sipping coffee and staring out the Eat Well's window.

"So whatta you think about what our neighbor down the road is doing?" asked Oscar.

"Which one? Since the vets moved in we've got a bunch of neighbors once more, sort of like it was in the old days when people didn't think they needed a thousand acres to make a living on a farm," said Fred.

"That's exactly what I'm talkin' about," said Oscar. "You read that piece in the paper about what John Wilson is doin'?"

"I did," said Fred. "What in hell has got into the man? I used to think if somebody had fifty cows it was probably too many. I just can't image a thousand cows in one place. That amounts to a lot of cow shit."

"You know, Fred," said Oscar, holding up a finger. "We got both sides of agriculture going on here in the valley."

"How so?"

"We've got these vets, most of them working from five to ten acres. And way on the other side"—Oscar extended his arm to its full reach—"we've got the likes of John Wilson planning on milking a thousand cows. Talk about your night and day. We've got it right here in the valley. How much more difference could there be? And dare I say it, these two different ways of farming—well, I'm a little concerned how they'll get along together, both being here at the same time in Settlers Valley."

Changing the subject, Fred asked, "You hear any more about the pipeline that's got its sights set on our valley?"

"Nope, nary a word. Hope they changed their mind about coming here. We got enough problems without having to deal with a damn pipeline. I've heard those buggers leak every so often and create a helluva mess when they do. Ruin the land. That's what they do. Ruin the land."

# 6

On a Friday afternoon in late April, a black Hertz rental car with Illinois plates rolled into Link Lake and parked on Main Street in one of the few remaining parking places. A tall, lanky fifty-something man with steel-gray hair climbed out of the rental, breathed deeply of the brisk April air, and stretched out his back. He was hungry and tired, having left Houston, Texas, earlier that morning and then flying to Chicago and driving to Link Lake without stopping. Halfway up the block-long Main Street, he spotted a sign: Eat Well Café: Home Cooking. He began walking in that direction, past the Link Lake Historical Society Museum, past the Link Lake Mercantile, past the nearly empty Ice Cream Shoppe, past the Used but Still Good resale store, past the post office, past the Link Lake State Bank. Across the street, he spotted a sign that read BTTL Grocery Cooperative. Barnes wondered what the letters stood for. He saw one couple and then another entering the Eat Well. He could smell fresh coffee and something being fried. It was a pleasant smell, reminding him of when he was a kid and his folks had taken him to a family restaurant for lunch on occasion.

Arriving at the Eat Well's door, he pulled it open and stepped inside. The place was nearly filled with people, some talking, some having a glass of beer or a glass of wine, but all of them eating. He saw a sign by the door: "Fish fry: all you can eat. With coleslaw and french fries. $7.50. Senior discount."

"How many?" the woman at the cash register asked. She had gray hair and wore glasses and a smile.

"Just one," the tall man said, wondering where she would find a place for him to sit in a room that looked filled.

He followed her to a table in the back of the room, near the swinging door to the kitchen. Two people were already sitting at the table set for four.

"Allen and Doris," the woman said, "would you mind if this gentleman joined you for supper?"

"Not at all," said Allen, who had just begun eating his plateful of fried fish. "Have a chair."

The tall man sat down. "My name is Richard," he said with a bit of a Texas drawl. "Richard Barnes, but everybody calls me Dick."

"Allen Towne," said the fellow across from him, extending his hand. "This here is my wife, Doris." Allen had big calloused hands that provided a firm handshake. Barnes liked that in a man.

"Hello," said Doris, quietly. She was just beginning to eat her fish as well.

"Ain't seen you around," said Allen. "You new to Link Lake?"

"Just got here," said Barnes. "Nice little town."

"Yup, it's a fair to middlin' place. Better than a bunch of towns that've been dryin' up the past few years. Not as good as some other towns. You here on business?"

"Not really," said Barnes. "I'm lookin' for someone."

"Lookin' for who?" asked Allen. He had a mouth full of fish.

"Young man name of C.J. Anderson. You know anybody with that name?"

"Jeez, everybody knows about C.J. Why you lookin' for him?"

"Saw an article in *USA Today* that said C.J. Anderson was a war veteran and a local hero."

A perky young waitress appeared in front of Barnes. She was blonde, short, and had a smile that filled up half of her face. "My name is Wendy, and I'll be your server. You ready to order?" she said.

27

"Oh, yes, ah'll have the special, same as these folks," said Barnes.

"You want coffee ta go with it?"

"Sure."

"You want cream?"

"No, just black," said Barnes.

Wendy wrote a few words on the little pad she carried and strode off to the kitchen, returning almost immediately with a coffee pot and cup. She put the cup down in front of Barnes and filled it, not spilling a drop.

"Thank you, ma'am," said Barnes.

"So you read an article about C.J.?" asked Allen.

"Ah did. He seems like quite a remarkable young man."

"Yeah, you could say that. But not ever-body around here likes what he's doin'."

"How so?" asked Barnes.

"Most of the folks here in Link Lake sorta like the town as it's been," said Allen.

"So, what does this that have to do with C.J. Anderson?" asked Barnes.

"I don't mean to sound harsh but he and them army vets what came with him have some far-out ideas. Really far-out," Towne said as he pierced another hunk of golden-brown fried cod.

Before Barnes could respond, a heaping plate of fried fish appeared in front of him, along with a bowl of coleslaw. He began eating. Barnes wondered what the other side of the C.J. Anderson story might be, but he didn't want to push too hard. Instead, in between bites of fried fish, he asked, "Do you know a place where I can spend the night?"

"Sure, just outta town you'll come onto the Link Lake Motel. Nothin' fancy, but clean with decent beds. Or so I'm told."

"Thank you, and do you know where I can find C.J. Anderson? I'd like to meet him."

"C.J. don't want no visitors. I know where he lives, but you wouldn't be welcome. You wanna talk with C.J., best you talk with his grandfather, Oscar Anderson."

"So how do I find the grandfather?" asked Barnes.

"Take County Highway A outta town west about three miles. Turn right on 15th road, travel down it for a mile or so and you'll come to Oscar's farm. His name is on his mailbox," said Towne.

# 7

*Ames County Argus*
LETTER TO THE EDITOR

This is in response to the several "letters to the editor" that have appeared in this paper in recent weeks. Several have been highly critical of what my fellow veterans and I have been doing since we moved to Link Lake a couple years ago. Some writers have called our Back to the Land Veterans a cult with secret meetings and strange celebrations. Others have said we are not patriotic because we are questioning long-held beliefs about the role of big business and especially the importance of industrial agriculture in our society. I fail to see the connection between big business and being patriotic. These comments especially hurt as all of us who are members of the Back to the Land Veterans group have served in this country's military and fought and were wounded in the name of the United States. We met at Walter Reed Hospital when we were recovering from our wounds.

To quell the rumors about who we are, what we do, and what we believe:

—Our group is made up of disabled military veterans.
—We are all small acreage farmers.

—We believe in sustainable agriculture, which means we farm our land so when we leave, it will be in better shape than it was when we acquired it.

—We are committed to protecting the environment.

—We believe in the importance and power of community.

—As a community, we work together, play together, and worship together.

—We generate as much of our own energy as possible, primarily through solar and wind power.

—We honor the land and all of its mystery and complexity.

—We hope other communities will see what we are doing and will try similar efforts.

I hope this helps answer some of the questions about the Back to the Land Veterans, who we are and what we do. Our various community events are open to everyone. Our BTTL Grocery Cooperative in Link Lake features our member-produced fruits, vegetables and meats, and much more. It is open to everyone. We want to be good neighbors, including with those who don't agree with what we are doing.

Signed, C.J. Anderson, Back to the Land Veterans, Link Lake

# 8

Fred Russo sat looking out the window at the Eat Well, occasionally glancing at his watch as he waited for Oscar to join him. Then he spotted him coming down Main Street, helped along by his walking stick. Once inside the Eat Well, Oscar made his way over to where Fred was seated and sat down opposite him. He tossed his John Deere cap on an empty chair and leaned his walking stick against the wall. He was out of breath.

"You're late," said Fred, not looking up from the menu in front of him.

"Whatta ya mean I'm late?" said Oscar, catching his breath. "It's only twenty after seven."

"You're still late. My old man said if you're not fifteen minutes early for something, you are late."

"Well, I'm not your old man," said Oscar, put out by his friend's early morning greeting. "You order yet?"

"I didn't. I was waiting for you."

"Well, I'm here now."

"Yes, you are," said Fred, smiling.

"You see the new sign on the Eat Well door?" asked Oscar.

"Can't say as I did," said Fred. "Don't pay much attention to signs these days, especially when I know where I am and where I'm going. What'd it say?"

"If you'd had your sleepy eyes open, you would have seen the sign that read 'We are a farm-to-table restaurant,'" said Oscar.

"I guess I did see it. Didn't have a clue what it meant," said Fred.

"Fred, you just ain't keepin' up what's happenin' in the world."

"So you gonna tell me what it means, what that there farm-to-table business is all about? Matter of fact, I don't see no farms crowdin' in on our table, or none of the other tables either."

"What it means is that this restaurant is buying most of its produce and meat from local producers. And you know what?"

"I bet you're gonna tell me whether I want to hear or not," said Fred.

"I am happy to report that the Back to the Land Veterans group has just signed a contract with the Eat Well to provide them with everythin' from chicken to lettuce and everythin' in between, everythin' that the vets are producin'," said Oscar.

"Well, that sounds purty good," said Fred.

Just then Wendy stopped by their table.

"You guys ready to order?" she asked, pencil and pad at the ready.

"Yeah, I guess so," muttered Oscar.

"What'll it be?" Wendy asked.

"I'll have two eggs over easy, some bacon, and whole wheat toast," said Oscar.

"And you?" Wendy said, pointing at Fred.

"I'll have the same, but sausage, not bacon. I heard bacon's not good for you."

"Coffee for both of you?"

Both men nodded their heads. "Black for me," said Fred.

"Black for me too," said Oscar.

Wendy hurried off.

"Fred, where'd you get the idea that bacon isn't good for you? You grew up eating bacon, and so did I," said Oscar.

"Read it someplace. The article said that bacon has lots of calories, lots of fat."

"Jeez, Fred, about everything we eat has lots of calories."

The two old friends sat quietly, staring out the restaurant window while they waited for their breakfasts to arrive. After a couple of minutes, Oscar said, "I've got somethin' important to share with you this morning."

"Really, somethin' important?"

"Yes, somethin' important," Oscar replied.

"And what might that be?" asked Fred as he picked up his coffee cup once more.

"I want to share some of my recent poetry," Oscar said quietly.

"I thought you quit writin' poetry, gave up on it. Took up somethin' more practical such as woodcarvin'. Now woodcarvin'—that is a fine hobby. Remember old George Maple? George was a woodcarver and pretty darn good at it too. He knew how to whittle a wooden chain with wooden links. Very impressive."

"Are you finished talkin' about woodcarvin'? asked Oscar.

"Well, yes, unless you would like some more information about this ancient and important hobby," answered Fred.

"You ever do any woodcarvin', Fred?"

"Nope never did. Might someday though. Just too busy these days to get into it."

"You wanna hear one of my new poems?" Oscar interrupted. "I wrote it last week. It's fresh out of my head."

"Fresh, huh. A fresh poem?"

"Yup, that's what I said. Brand spankin' new," answered Oscar.

Just at that moment, Wendy came with their breakfasts.

"Can we wait with the poetry until we've worked our way around these eggs?" asked Fred.

"I expect so. Don't want eggs to get cold."

After a few minutes, Oscar wiped his chin with a napkin and then reached into his pocket for a lined piece of paper with handwriting on each line. "You ready for my new poem, Fred?"

"Thought maybe you'd forgotten about the poem," Fred answered.

"So, you really don't want to hear it, do you?" Oscar said, miffed by his friend's comment.

"No, no, not at all, go ahead. Read your poem. I'm all ears," said Fred. "My hearin' aids are even workin' this morning."

"As the community's professor of poetry, I am pleased to say that you are the first person to hear this new poem," began Oscar in a serious voice.

"So you're gonna keep callin' yourself a professor of poetry— you're no damn professor. You never spent a day at any college."

"Yeah, that's right, but it doesn't stop me from being a professor of poetry. Has a nice ring to it, wouldn't you say?" asked Oscar. A big smile cut across his face.

"It has a ring, sort of like when you strike a hammer against a broken bell."

"Now, Fred, haven't you a little sense of humor?" asked Oscar, still smiling.

"What's humor got to do with proclaimin' you are a professor of poetry?"

Deciding to drop the professor discussion, Oscar said, "So how'd you like to hear the poem I've been workin' on?"

"Do I have a choice?" said Fred.

"Okay," said Oscar as he cleared his throat and began reading in his strong baritone voice.

*The Land*
We walk on it,
Dig in it, and
Build on it
We bury our dead in it,
We bury our trash in it.
The scientists call it soil.
Housewives call it dirt when they find it in their kitchens.
For the Native People, it is sacred.

Lest we forget, and we often do,
Our food comes from the land,
Much of what we wear comes from the land.
All of us, young and old,
Farmer and city person,
We must come to respect the land,
revere and care for it.
When there is no more land,
There will be no more people.

Oscar folded up the paper and put it in his pocket. "So what do you think, Fred?"

"About what?"

"Jeez, about my poem?"

"Purty good," said Fred.

"You really like it?" asked Oscar, smiling.

"Well, I don't wanna go that far, but it's purty good. Has lots of important words."

"I considered readin' it at the school forest gatherin' the other day."

"Why didn't you?"

"This poem's about the land. The school forest program was about trees," said Oscar.

"Trees are a part of the land," Fred said.

"I guess they are. Guess they are at that," Oscar replied. "Kilmer poem was about trees. That was a good poem for that day."

"Yes, it was," said Fred. "Yes, it was. Trees are lookin' really good at the school forest."

"Hope they always look that good," said Oscar.

With coffee refills, the two old friends sat quietly for a bit, enjoying each other's company. Oscar thought of one of his father's sayings: "Don't forget how important it is to just sit awhile and think, or not think."

"I'm gonna try somethin' new," he said, breaking the silence. "Something related to my role as professor of poetry here in Settlers Valley. The idea came to me in the night. Right out of the blue. My mind was blank and then it was filled with this new idea. Took over my thinkin', it did."

"So what's this 'it came out of the blue' idea that filled your head in the dark of night?" asked Fred.

"Don't be sarcastic, Fred. This is one of my better ideas."

"Okay, what is it?"

"As the Settlers Valley Professor of Poetry . . . ," began Oscar.

Fred rolled his eyes and motioned to the waitress to bring more coffee.

"As the Settlers Valley Professor of Poetry, I am going to clean up my old barn and in the space, I am organizin' the Red Barn Writers' Workshop," said Oscar proudly.

"You what?" said Fred, a little too loud.

"You heard me, Fred. I am organizin' a writers' workshop."

"You mean where students come and learn about writing? That what you mean?" asked Fred.

"You got it, Fred. Doesn't that have a nice ring to it, Red Barn Writers' Workshop?"

"Who's it for?"

"The disabled veterans here in the valley. I read that writin' stuff down can help troubled people heal. I want to give it a try. See what happens," said Oscar.

"Who you gonna ask to do the teachin'?" asked Fred. "For somethin' like this to work, you'll need a good teacher."

"Right you are, Fred. I've got a good teacher in mind."

"Who?" asked Fred.

"Me. After all, I am the Settlers Valley Professor of Poetry."

"Good God, Oscar, now you've really gone over the cliff," said Fred.

"Maybe, maybe so. But I wanna give it a shot. See how it goes," said Oscar.

"Well, about all I can say, Oscar, is good luck. You're gonna need it," said Fred.

The two old men continued to finish their breakfasts.

"Had a visitor yesterday," said Oscar.

"Who was it? That lady preacher? I've heard that she's been makin' the rounds these days, stoppin' by veterans' farms like your grandson's. She hasn't stopped by my place yet. Wish she would. She seems to be gettin' under the skin of old Preacher Jacob John Jacob at the Church of the Holy Redeemed. It's high time somebody got under his skin. He's the most pious old bugger I've ever run in to."

"Nope, it wasn't the lady preacher that stopped by," said Oscar.

"Who then? The Watkins man doesn't come around anymore. No feed salesmen—you ain't got any animals at your place, except for your old dog."

"Well, if you'd shut up for a minute, I'll tell you who it was," said Oscar.

Fred ran a hand across his mouth, indicating that he had zipped his mouth shut.

"Fellow's name was Richard Barnes," said Oscar.

"I don't know anybody with that name."

"Why should you? He's from Houston."

"Houston, Minnesota?" asked Fred.

"No. Houston, Texas."

"He's a long way from home," said Fred. "What'd he want?"

"Said he saw an article in that *USA Today* newspaper. Said he wanted to talk with C.J., but someone had told him that C.J. was not keen on talkin' to strangers, especially about his war experiences. Said he had lost a son in Afghanistan; said his son's name was Josh. Said he was interested in learnin' more about disabled veterans like C.J. and his friends who are livin' here in Ames County and workin' on small farms."

"What's he wanna know?" asked Fred.

"Well, here's the thing. This Barnes fellow said he might wanna invest some money in what C.J. and his group are doing. He didn't say how much. But I got the idea from how he talked he had a fair amount of cash. I didn't ask how he'd gotten it. None of my business."

"Sounds a little fishy to me," said Fred. "You sure this guy is on the up and up and not just some sick character who wants to take advantage of disabled veterans?"

"He talked like an honest man who wanted to help out a group that needed some help. He told me how important it is for farmers to be takin' care of their land, to be doin' what he called sustainable agriculture. The kind of farmin' that C.J. is promotin'. He even gave me a phone number to call in Houston, where if I had any questions, I could ask. He said I might be skeptical of his offer and I should be sure I was comfortable with him," offered Oscar.

"You called the number yet?" asked Fred.

"Nope, I ain't called yet. I wanted your take on this first."

"What if the number you call is a fake, a setup?"

"I thought about that. If I call, I'll find out if he is for real and try to find out if he's who he says he is, and that he will do what he says he will do."

"Did he say how much money he wants to contribute?" asked Fred.

"Nope, but he did say that the way industrial agriculture is headed these days, in short order the land in this country will be ruined," said Oscar.

"I think you'd better make the call," said Fred.

# 9

Oscar punched in the numbers on his phone. He waited while he heard the phone ring three times, and then a woman's voice with a Texas accent answered. Oscar heard, "Herman Barnes Family Foundation. How can ah help y'all?"

"What's the name of your company?" asked Oscar in what he hoped was a friendly tone.

"It's not a company. These are the offices of the Herman Barnes Family Foundation."

"My name is Oscar Anderson, and I live in Wisconsin near a town called Link Lake. I met a fellow the other day by the name of Richard Barnes. Does he work for this here foundation you mentioned?"

"Wall, yes, sir, he sort of does. This is his family's foundation. He's ma boss. How can I help you?"

All Oscar could think to say was, "Is he there today?"

"No, Mr. Barnes is not in today," the receptionist said. "So how can I help?"

Oscar was pondering if the receptionist was for real or if this was all part of some scam that Richard Barnes had instigated.

"What can you tell me about the Herman Barnes Family Foundation?" asked Oscar.

"Well, the foundation is not very big—I'm the only employee. We make grants to worthy causes. Are y'all interested in applyin' for a grant?"

"Well, no. I'm . . ." Oscar hesitated. "I'm interested in learnin' a bit more about your boss."

"Well, y'all should talk to him about that. But I can say, he's one fine gentleman. He works hard," the receptionist said. "He gives me a bonus each year at Christmas, and lets me take the day off for my birthday each year."

Oscar began feeling both comfortable and uncomfortable. He was comfortably assured that Richard Barnes was the real thing and uncomfortable about prying into his personal life.

"You've been most helpful," he said, deciding to end the conversation. "Thank you and you have a great day."

Oscar hung up the phone. He thought, *Now what? Sounds like Link Lake and the disabled veteran farmers in Settlers Valley are about to have a big supporter. But for what? And why? Money usually complicates things rather than making them easier.* He remembered one of his father's many sayings: "The most important things in life, like a sunset, a good friend, and a lovin' family, can't be bought with money."

# 10

For two weeks, Oscar swept, scrubbed, and otherwise tidied up his big red barn's hayloft—a vast expanse of open space where tons of hay had been stored for many years. As he worked, his mind moved back to the days when his father farmed with horses and Oscar was but a little kid. He remembered haying season, one of his favorite times. If the spring rains had come regularly and there had been plenty of warm sunny days, haying season would start in mid-June, when Oscar's father would cut a big field of alfalfa hay, maybe twenty acres. He waited for the hay to dry a bit, then raked it into long threads that Oscar helped pile into bunches. Bunching the hay allowed it to dry some more. When Oscar's father decided the hay was dry enough, but not so dry that the alfalfa leaves would shatter, he hitched the team to the hay wagon. Oscar and his dad pitched the hay bunches on the wagon until it was as high as their three-tine forks would reach. Then they drove to the barn. There they unloaded the hay using a mechanical hayfork that lifted the loose hay from the wagon and deposited it on either side end of the barn in the haymows.

As Oscar worked, he occasionally smelled a hint of stored hay, bringing back this cascade of memories. The cleaning task had become a memory trip, not at all unpleasant, even though a couple of decades of no use had left behind lots of dust, cobwebs, and pigeon droppings.

Oscar borrowed some folding tables and chairs from the Link Lake Library and hand-painted a little sign that he hung on the barn wall: Red Barn Writers' Workshop. Before the first meeting, he met with Pastor Vicki to get her ideas about how the workshop might benefit the vets who struggled with PTSD. Oscar invited C.J. and Pastor Vicki to the first writers' workshop, which he had planned as a two-hour session the following Saturday. He also asked them to spread the word among the Back to the Land Veterans.

The Saturday for the workshop was a beautiful day in May with a blue sky, puffy clouds, and the temperature in the low seventies. Oscar knew how uncomfortably hot it could get in the hayloft. But on this day, a slight breeze flowing through the big hayloft door would keep everyone comfortable.

Oscar was concerned that the day was too beautiful and that the vets would choose to stay home and work rather than spend two hours in a writing workshop. He was pleasantly surprised. Everyone in the Back to Land Veterans group came, except Randy Budwell, who had recently left the valley. Pastor Vicki had visited Randy's farm a couple of times and noted that he wasn't doing well. She knew that he had a drinking problem, but she thought she had been making progress with him. Apparently not. Last time she visited him late one morning, he was still in bed. The vegetables he had planted were mostly overrun with weeds, and his little cabin, which his fellow vets had helped him build, was a mess.

"Sit wherever you'd like," said Oscar as the veterans began arriving. He had arranged for four people to be at each table. When everyone was seated, Oscar welcomed them, and said, "I'll do a little talkin', but mostly this is your workshop. Our focus will be on your stories."

"I wanna begin by talking for a minute or two about journalin'," he continued. "Any of you keep a journal?"

C.J.'s hand went up.

"C.J., are you willin' to tell us a little about your journal, how often you write in it, maybe a little about what you write in it, if you're comfortable doin' that?" asked Oscar.

43

C.J. hesitated. "I write in it when . . . when, I feel like it," he said.

"Can you tell us anythin' about what you write?" asked Oscar.

"I'd . . . I'd rather not say," said C.J.

"Thank you," Oscar said. "One of the rules of this writin' workshop is no one shares anythin' he's not comfortable sharin'."

Oscar went on to explain that he had kept a journal for more than forty years. He told how he described the weather each day, the temperature, and whether it had rained. He mentioned that at the beginning of each day, he thought about what happened the previous day, whether it was good or bad, and wrote about what he thought was important. If he met someone he found interesting, or encountered someone who ticked him off, or if he heard a good story—he wrote all of this down. Oscar ended with an assignment for the members of the group.

"I want to encourage each of you to buy a notebook and try some journalin'. Next time we meet, we'll talk about how it went for you. Even if you think journalin' is the dumbest idea that ever came down the country road, I'd like you to give it a try. Any questions?" He looked around the room and saw a mixture of expressions on the vets' faces.

"Okay, enough about journalin'. In front of you, you will find a blank sheet of paper," said Oscar. "Here's what I want you to do. Think back to when you were ten or twelve years old. Think of the house or apartment you lived in at that time. Using that big sheet of paper, I'd like you to sketch the floor plan for your home. Put in all the rooms, put the furniture in the rooms, note the people associated with each room, indicate the pictures on the wall, the smells and sounds you remember associated with each room. You have twenty minutes."

Oscar had gotten the idea of this exercise from Pastor Vicki, who said she had used it with other disabled vets. For most of the vets, drawing the house plan of the home where they grew up brought back pleasant memories. "Many of these vets, especially those suffering from PTSD, have trouble thinking happy thoughts," Pastor Vicki had told him.

When the twenty minutes were up, Oscar said, "Okay, now share your drawin' with the person sittin' next to you."

Even Oscar was surprised by how readily the vets took to the task, and what joy he saw on their faces as they shared a slice of their childhoods with another person. The old barn was abuzz with happy voices. Next Oscar said, "Now, look at your drawin', and write a story about somethin' that happened in one of those rooms when you were a kid. You have ten minutes."

This time all was quiet. So quiet that Oscar could hear the sound of the spring breeze as it collided with the old barn. Each vet was writing a story. Remembering an event. Thinking about family members and details of their lives at an earlier time.

Then they began sharing their stories, stories about happenings that took place in their growing up homes, memories of Christmas mornings, stories about Thanksgiving and the wonderful kitchen smells associated with that celebration, tales of playing tricks on siblings. Funny stories. Sad stories. Short stories, longer ones.

When the group members finished sharing their stories, Oscar said, "Your assignment before the next workshop meeting is to write about someone who made a difference in your life—someone who helped you, or someone who challenged you. Any questions? Okay. See you next time."

# II

*Ames County Argus*
Letters to the Editor
NEWS FROM THE LINK LAKE
PEOPLE'S CHURCH

Dear Editor,

This is in response to those living in Ames County and
especially to those living in and around Link Lake who have
asked about the Link Lake People's Church: who we are, what we
stand for, and where we came from. Let me start with the third
question first. I served for five years in the U.S. Army as a
chaplain, with two tours in Afghanistan. I saw young men and
women coming to me with questions, often life-and-death
questions. I saw death and maiming. I saw fear and guilt. I saw
hatred and love, caring and sharing. I was wounded along with
hundreds of others.

When I left the army two years ago, I did not leave behind my
commitment to help those in need. I looked around this great
country in search of a place where I could start a church and do
the work I have committed my life to doing. I stumbled on the
article in *Reader's Digest* about C.J. Anderson and his fellow
disabled veterans and their return to the land as an approach to
healing. I was struck by the writer's comment that not only did

these young men and women see the land helping them heal but they also recognized that their approach to farming would also heal the land. As we heal the land, we heal ourselves. Powerful words for a torn society.

Using my savings, and the savings of several of my friends, I purchased the former Lutheran church building in Link Lake. Our church has some 150 members at this writing and is nondenominational. We are not part of any church hierarchy. We do not care if you are or were followers of another religion. We do not care if you never attended a church in your life, or you attended every Sunday. Everyone is welcome to participate in and be part of the Link Lake People's Church congregation. No examination. No questions asked.

Here are some of our beliefs:

—We are a church of hope for those who have lost all hope.
—We are a church that cares, especially for those who need special caring.
—We are a church with great admiration and concern for nature and the land.
—We believe that much can be learned by being close to nature.
—We are a church without ancient dogma and rules.
—We believe that good always triumphs over evil.
—We believe in the power of critical thinking and the joy of creative thought.
—We believe in understanding the past, and drawing the best from it, but not allowing the past to hinder what we must do today.
—We believe in a higher power, some may call it God, which can nourish and sustain us in good times and in bad.
—We believe in the importance of self-reliant individuals, but at the same time we believe in the power of community,

where self-reliant individuals work together for the common good.

—We are a church of the people and for the people.

Signed, Victoria Emerson, Pastor, Link Lake People's Church

The next week, the following letter appeared.

*Ames County Argus*
REVERED JACOB RESPONDS TO
PASTOR EMERSON'S LETTER

Dear Editor,

I am astonished and profoundly troubled by what I read in your "Letters to the Editor" last week—the letter from Pastor Emerson. I am perplexed that you would allow such a letter to be published. You must realize that you are supporting the Antichrist by publishing such drivel. It's clear to me that Victoria Emerson is no pastor but is likely a tool of the devil. How can a church be called a church with no mention of the Bible as its guide? How can a church be called a church with no mention of sin and salvation? No mention of the second coming? No discussion of heaven and hell? No mention of the end times? No mention of the cross?

I call upon my fellow believers in the Word to help abolish this so-called church, which is an abomination and should not be in the Link Lake community.

Signed, Jacob John Jacob, Pastor, Church of the Holy Redeemed

On Sunday evening, three days after Pastor Jacob's letter appeared in the *Ames County Argus*, Pastor Emerson lay awake thinking of her colleague's letter. How difficult it was to even consider him a colleague after seeing the bitter words that he had written. She was both surprised and disappointed that in what appeared to be a lovely community there could exist such bitterness toward something different, something new—the People's Church. She had invested all of her savings and those of her friends. She borrowed heavily to buy the building, which included a large community room open for any and all community events, no matter if they belonged to the church or not.

Pastor Vicki lived in the back of the church in a little apartment that consisted of a bedroom, bath, and a combination kitchen, dining, and living room. It was small but comfortable. As she lay thinking about what she should do, if anything, in response to Pastor Jacob's tirade, she caught a whiff of smoke. Had she forgotten to blow out the candles she had used as a part of the Sunday afternoon service? To her surprise, it had been nearly a full house packed with veterans and their families, including many she had not previously seen in the church but knew from her visits going farm to farm introducing herself and inviting them to attend services. There were others in the crowd that she had not met before. The church could seat about 150 people, and nearly every seat was taken. She remembered how two years ago when the church first opened its doors, if twenty-five people showed up she considered it a crowd. What the church was doing, and what she was trying to do, especially with the disabled veterans, was catching on. She was pleased. But then she thought about the letter and the pushback from Pastor Jacob. How many others in this community felt as he did about the People's Church?

Pastor Vicki caught the smell of smoke again and decided she had better get up and check to see if she had left some candles burning. When she opened the door separating her little apartment from the church proper, she saw flames licking at the back wall of the church. The church was on fire. She hurried back to her apartment, grabbed her cell phone, and called 911. While she waited for the volunteer fire department to arrive, she gathered up church records, song sheets, and her computer equipment and carried them outside. As she did that, she caught a whiff of gasoline.

Fifteen minutes later, the fire truck arrived. Firefighters moved swiftly to spray water on the church, which was now wholly engulfed in yellow flames with thick black smoke rising from the roof. The Link Lake Volunteer Fire Department was no match for what was now a roaring inferno of destruction. Pastor Vicki stood by watching and trying not to cry. All of her hopes, to say nothing of her meager savings, were destroyed. The fire department kept the nearby homes from catching fire, but the church was a total loss.

With red and blue lights flashing and the siren screaming, Ames County sheriff Floyd Jansen arrived. Jansen, in his early fifties, stood about six feet five, weighed about 275 pounds, and took no guff from anyone. He had garnered the respect of nearly everyone in the county, no matter what their political or religious persuasion.

"Is the pastor here?" Jansen asked in a loud, commanding voice. A volunteer firefighter pointed to where Pastor Vicki was sitting, away from the flames and smoke. Hitching up his ever-present pistol belt, Jansen walked over to the pastor. He put his hand on her shoulder, and she looked up. In a quiet voice, he said, "Can we talk, or would you rather wait until morning?"

Pastor Vicki rubbed her eyes with her handkerchief and sat up straight.

"What can you tell me about this?" the sheriff asked.

Pastor Vicki ran over the sequence of events from when she first smelled smoke until now.

"Do you have any idea of how the fire might have started?" asked the sheriff.

"No, no, I don't. When we took over this building, we had the wiring brought up to date. We also installed a new furnace," Vicki said, trying to hold back tears she felt welling up once more.

"Anything else you remember, even if you think it might not be important?" the sheriff asked.

"I did smell gasoline," Vicki said. "Do you suppose somebody started this fire on purpose? Could that be true? Here in Link Lake, somebody would start a fire in a church?"

"People do strange things for even stranger reasons. We'll send a team of arson experts over here tomorrow when it cools off. They'll be able to declare whether somebody set fire to your church or something else happened," the sheriff said.

"Thank you," Pastor Vicki said as the tears began flowing once more.

By this time, several of the veterans and others in the community had heard about the fire and arrived to offer their help. They loaded what Pastor Vicki had saved from the fire into their cars. Before the fire was entirely out, Red Cross responders arrived at the scene, offering hot coffee to volunteer firefighters and trying to console Pastor Vicki, who sat on the office chair she had saved from the fire, quietly sobbing, holding her face in her hands.

# 12

The two old friends sat opposite each other at the Eat Well, neither saying anything for a long time. Oscar finally said, "Fred, what's happenin' to our community? What's happenin' to Link Lake? This is not us. This is not who we are."

"I heard on the radio what you probably heard, Oscar. Sheriff Jansen has declared the site of the Link Lake People's Church a crime scene. It didn't take long for the arson people to decide that someone had deliberately started the fire. They even found the empty charred gasoline can."

"But who would do that? Who would deliberately burn down a church?" asked Oscar.

"Well, if anybody can get to the bottom of this, Sheriff Jansen can do it. How'd Ames County ever elect such a competent guy, after a couple of sheriffs that seemed more interested in getting reelected than doin' their jobs?" said Fred.

"Yup, Jansen's a competent guy," Oscar agreed. "If anyone can figure out who set the fire, he can. By the way, did you read the tirade that the Reverend Jacob John Jacob wrote in the *Argus* last week?"

"I did," said Fred. "The radio guy said he tried to interview Jacob about the fire and his letter to the editor, but the reverend had nothin' to say other than: "The fire was God's will.""

"I remember," began Oscar as he sat down his coffee cup, "when the churches in Link Lake—at one time we had a Catholic church, a

Lutheran church, a Presbyterian church, a Baptist church, a Methodist church—when everybody got along with everybody else, no matter if they believed things a little differently. In a way it's too bad those churches lost membership and closed down. People who belonged to those churches now go to the Willow River churches, leaving us with the Church of the Holy Redeemed and Link Lake People's Church."

"Oscar, did I hear right? Is Pastor Vicki stayin' with you?"

"Well, she has to live someplace and although the Link Lake Motel is okay for a night or two, it's no place for someone to take up any kind of permanent residence," said Oscar. "I've got some extra rooms—besides, it's good to have someone around. I talk to my dog a lot, but old Rex doesn't talk back much. I think Rex likes the pastor living there too. I think he does."

"Well, a few folks are beginnin' to talk. They know you are living alone out there on your farm in Settlers Valley, and now this young woman has moved in with you. A few tongues are waggin' and a few fingers are pointin'," said Fred.

"Let their damn tongues wag and their nosey fingers point. By God, I just figured it was the right thing to do. I didn't want her up and movin' away from here. My grandson and the other disabled vets need her. They really do. She could find another community for a church. So I invited her to stay with me until she raises enough money to rebuild," said Oscar, sounding a bit miffed about the direction the conversation was going.

"Is it true that Pastor Vicki plans to hold services in your old barn?" asked Fred.

"Yup, since I've already cleaned it up for the Red Barn Writers, the place looks pretty darn good. It's a good place for the professor of poetry to hold forth," said Oscar. "Seems appropriate that a bunch of beginnin' farmers would learn about writin' in an old barn, wouldn't you say? And likewise, a barn seems a good place to worship too."

"So you're still on that 'professor of poetry' kick?" said Fred.

"Yup, I am. You wouldn't think anybody would study writin' with an old retired farmer who scarcely scraped through school. But they might come if the teacher is a professor of somethin' or other," said Oscar.

"Oscar, you are so full of it. Every damn one of those vets knows you are no more or less than an old retired farmer," said Fred.

"Well, thank you for those words of support," said Oscar.

Changing the subject, Fred said, "Ain't you worried that somebody might come by and set your barn afire like they did with the church?" asked Fred.

"Nope, not worried a bit," said Oscar. "I've got Mazzie and Rex lookin' out for me."

"Who?"

"Rex—he might be old, but that big old collie dog still knows how to sound an alarm when somethin' doesn't seem just right there on the farm. And Mazzie is my old double-barrel 12-gauge shotgun. Nope, not worried. Not a bit. In fact, I'm kind of lookin' forward to my old barn bein' put back to use. When I offered the barn to Pastor Vicki, she began cryin', she was so grateful," said Oscar.

"Is she gonna rebuild?" asked Fred.

"She says she will. She had some insurance on the church, and the disabled vets have started a fund drive. The pastor said she'd put a story up on Facebook, talking about the disabled vets, and how they'd come to depend on the church, and how folks, if they were so inclined, could donate money toward buildin' a new church."

"I don't know much about that Facebook thing. Don't believe I've ever watched it. Can't imagine watchin' somethin' on that internet is gonna haul in any money."

"Well, we'll see," said Oscar. "Pastor said lots of folks hook up with the internet and Facebook. I don't know much about it either. It'll be a tough go all right, but I'm impressed with Pastor Vicki. She's been around the tree enough times to know how to get things done. If anyone can build another church, Pastor Vicki will."

"I hope so. Her People's Church was a breath of fresh air in our community. No question about it. She was workin' hard tryin' to get us all talkin' to each other, even though we don't agree on lots of things. And besides, what she's doin' for these disabled veterans—well, that's pretty darn special," said Fred.

"Say, Fred, you gonna enter some of your famous rhubarb wine in the competition at the upcoming rhubarb festival?" said Oscar, changing the subject.

"Thinkin' about it. I just might do it, too. Cuz I know you'll be bringin' that stuff you call rhubarb wine. I might be about to gather a blue ribbon on mine this year," said Fred, smiling from ear to ear.

"Well, that's it. I was thinkin' of takin' a pass on enterin' this year. Last year's wine turned out dang good, though, and hearin' what you just said, I will beat your wine for the blue ribbon hands down. No competition from your product," said Oscar.

"Says you, old-timer. Says you," Fred retorted.

"Well, you probably didn't remember, being the old guy that you are, that my dad once made rhubarb wine, and I have followed his recipe down to the last little bit of yeast. It even looks good, not all cloudy as it is some years. Got quite a kick to it too."

"Good for you, Oscar. You'll need all the help you can get if you want your wine to compete with the superior product that I've been makin' for the past twenty-five years," said Fred.

"Twenty-five years, huh? That's a long time tryin' to learn how to make a superior wine product," said Oscar.

"You'll see, Oscar. We'll let the judges decide," said Fred.

"I remember what Pa used to say when he was makin' wine," said Oscar.

"And that would be?" asked Fred.

"Wine a little, laugh a lot," said Oscar, smiling broadly.

"Jeez, Oscar, that the best you got?" said Fred. He was chuckling.

# 13

The first oak leaves of spring had just begun to show in the woodlot in the back of Oscar Anderson's farmstead on a sunny May Sunday. Lazy white clouds rolled across a blue sky. Dandelions showed yellow in their unique way and reminded Oscar that spring was once more here. Never once did he try to kill a dandelion in his lawn.

Cars began arriving and parking in what had once been the barnyard. Folding chairs stood in rows where once bales of hay had been piled. Oscar had helped Pastor Vicki cobble together a makeshift podium from a pile of used boards. She told him that she had used much worse when she held church services as a chaplain in Afghanistan. Promptly at 1:00 p.m. Pastor Vicki looked out on a barn full of people. Every chair had been taken and people were standing in the back and along the sides. She recognized the veterans she had been working with, but there were many more faces she didn't recognize.

In a loud, clear voice, she began. "Thank you all for coming. It is a beautiful day, in more ways than the warmth and promise of spring, which is on full display this afternoon. Someone once said, 'Out of tragedy good often emerges.'

"Today we are experiencing some of that good as we try to rid our minds of the bad. We remember the destruction of our beloved church, which we had hoped would not only provide a place for gathering and reflection but would also serve as a beacon to bring together people of different thoughts and opinions, different hopes and aspirations.

"Let's focus on the good for a moment. Let's give a round of applause to Oscar Anderson. He's sitting right here in front. Hold up your hand, Oscar. This is Oscar's barn. We are using it at no charge. These are the school's chairs, also at no charge." A loud round of applause began that echoed just a little in the enormous space that once was piled high with hay.

"Where do we go from here? Several people have asked. Will we build another church? The answer is yes, but it will take some time to raise the necessary funds. We hope that before winter we'll have a warm place to gather. Another question I am hearing: How do we confront Pastor Jacob, whose letter to the editor a few weeks ago may have prompted someone to burn our beloved church?

"I have tried to talk with Pastor Jacob. I suggested we have coffee together and talk about our common interests—what we can agree on even though our disagreements are wide and deep. He does not want to talk. Pastor Jacob also let me know that no woman should have the right to be called a pastor. 'Pastors are men,' he said emphatically.

"I don't want to judge Pastor Jacob; he has his own demons to wrestle with. But I also don't want to stand quietly by, with our church building a pile of ashes and many of our hopes dashed. I suggest we move forward with hope and determination. That we build a new church. That we continue to seek reconciliation with those whose beliefs are different from ours. We will not—let me repeat—we will not criticize the Church of the Holy Redeemed and its devoted members. We will not make disparaging comments about Pastor Jacob. We are a church of hope for those who have lost all hope. We are a church that cares, especially for those who need special caring. We are a church with great admiration and concern for nature and the land, and we believe that good will always triumph over evil. We are a church of the people and for the people. These are words we have proclaimed in our church's statement of beliefs. We must not forget them. We must remove from our thinking such words as hate and revenge, even though I have heard some of the members of our congregation use these words when talking about the Church of the Holy Redeemed.

"We must move forward holding our heads high, demonstrating our beliefs through our actions." After a brief pause, she continued. "As you all know, our practice in this church is to give everyone an opportunity to say a few words at our gathering times. We are a church of the people and that means we all are to share, as we are so inclined. So who will be first?"

Oscar Anderson stood up and made his way to the podium. Pastor Vicki sat on a nearby chair.

"First," Oscar began, "welcome to my barn and thank you all for comin' here on this beautiful spring day." He was interrupted by loud clapping as the congregation showed its appreciation to Oscar for offering his big old dairy barn for this new use.

"It's a troublin' time," Oscar continued. "Our community is divided. I'm eighty-five years old and never in all my years have I been pushed to take up sides—to believe one way and to criticize those who don't believe as I do. This is new for Link Lake. This is new for Settlers Valley. I remember what the Link Lake community was like fifty years ago. At the time we were made up of Irish, German, Welsh, Polish, Bohemian, English, and Norwegian families, and even a Russian family. People attended Baptist, Lutheran, Methodist, Presbyterian, and Catholic churches—some attended no churches at all. We supported one another's fundraisers, chili suppers, and craft shows, and we attended all the weddin' dances. We didn't try to convince one another that what we believed was right and what the other person believed was wrong. We worked together. We shared stores. We learned from one another."

Oscar paused and shuffled through the few notes that he had brought with him. He looked up to the attentive audience and continued. "Our Link Lake Community is sick, but I see healin' in our future. This church, the Link Lake People's Church, is a healin' church. We can, and we must help our community heal. We must move past finger pointin' and hateful words. Each one of us, young and old, man and woman, adult and child must help by workin' together, sharin', and carin' for one another, no matter what our differences," Oscar concluded before returning to his seat.

The congregation erupted in applause, and then everyone was standing, continuing to clap.

"Does anyone else have some words for us today?" Pastor Vicki asked. She was rubbing a tear from her eye.

C.J. made his way to the podium. "First," he said, looking at his grandfather, "I've told Grandpa this several times, but I've never mentioned it in public. Today I want to do that. As the other veterans in this audience are aware, it was my grandpa Oscar Anderson's idea for me to come to Settlers Valley and become a farmer. It was Grandpa Oscar's knowledge about the land and its healing powers that I didn't know until I began digging in the dirt and discovered how important working the land has been for me. I returned from Afghanistan with one good leg and a bad attitude. When I arrived at Grandpa Oscar's farm, I was a miserable, sorry sight. Just ask him, he'll tell you." C.J. glanced at his grandfather, who was slowing nodding.

"I'm not entirely well, not entirely whole—yet. But I'm working on it. My farm and my fellow farmers in the Back to the Land Veterans group and this church are helping." C.J. returned to his seat as the congregation once more applauded.

Pastor Vicki glanced at her watch and asked, "Does anyone have a favorite song you'd like to sing as part of our service today?" She looked out over the crowd. A hand went up way in the back. It was Fred Russo.

59

Fred slowly made his way to the front of the room. He was wearing a bright red shirt and his "going to town" bib overalls. In a loud, clear voice, Fred said, "I'd like to sing for you one of my favorite old-time songs, 'Amazing Grace.' You are all welcome to join me."

Oscar was more than a little surprised to see Fred ambling toward the front of the group. He remembered how, when Fred's wife was living, the two of them would sing duets at their church. After Fred's wife died, he had vowed to never sing again. And he hadn't, to the best of Oscar's knowledge. Until right now. In front of this gathering, with a hint of stored alfalfa hay still in the air, Fred smiled at Pastor Vicki and in a loud, clear baritone voice began singing.

Amazing grace! How sweet the sound
That saved a wretch like me!
I once was lost, but now am found;
Was blind, but now I see.

As Fred sang, tears began rolling down his face, but he continued on, soon joined by many others in the group who had remembered the old-time favorite.

T'was grace that taught my heart to fear,
And grace my fears relieved;
How precious did that grace appear
The hour I first believed!

As Fred continued singing, Oscar suddenly heard his dog, Rex, barking. The big collie never barked unless he noted some danger, some threat. And then came gunshots, three of them, loud enough so that Fred quit singing and everyone rushed outside in time to see a pickup truck roaring off, already too far away to catch the number on the license plate.

Oscar spotted Rex limping toward him. The dog had been shot in the leg. "I was a medic in the army," a churchgoer said. "I've got a first aid kit in my car." He rushed off and soon returned with bandages and antiseptic. "It's only a graze," said the medic. "He'll be good as new in a week or so."

"Who could have done this?" lamented Oscar as he petted his old four-footed friend.

"Who could be so mean that they would shoot a dog?" Pastor Vicki had her hand on Oscar's shoulder. Concern was written all over her face, but no words came from her mouth.

# 14

*Ames County Argus*
EDITORIAL BY BILL BAXTER, MANAGING EDITOR

When we should be celebrating the coming of spring and the planting season on our farms, something dark and menacing is occurring in our community. It likely has been bubbling beneath the surface for several years, but now, this thing that I don't quite know how to name has surfaced and it isn't pretty.

I'm not one to get involved with religious differences of opinion. I learned that from my father, who preceded me as editor of this newspaper. He learned the business from his father, who also ran this paper at one time. What my father said was, "Avoid discussing religion. You'll only get into trouble."

Today, I am violating that rule, but what is occurring in the Link Lake community needs airing out and the problem appears to begin with religion. First a little history. The Village of Link Lake was founded by a preacher, Increase Joseph Link, who with his small band of followers found their way to Ames County and Link Lake in 1852, when Native Americans lived freely on these lands. Pastor Increase Joseph, as people called him, promoted a religion not too different from Pastor Victoria Emerson's Link Lake People's Church.

Pastor Increase Joseph's sermons are stored at the Link Lake Historical Society. Consider this passage, written in 1852:

"We are all part of the land, have been and forever will be. As farmers, it is our God-given task to care for the land, to till it, nourish it, protect it, and above all give it respect. In return, the land will feed us, embrace us, and give us the joy that comes from a bountiful harvest. It is our connection to the land that nourishes our souls and gives us a glimpse into God's wonderful creation."

Using slightly different words, Pastor Emerson's church seems pointed in a similar direction, building on the theme that as we take care of the land, the land will take care of us. Pastor Emerson, herself a wounded war veteran, believes that the veterans who belong to her church and till the fields of Settlers Valley are healing as they work to heal the land.

Pastor Emerson's goal is a noble one. She—along with C.J. Anderson and his grandfather, Oscar Anderson—is advocating a back to the land movement. By working on the land, the Back to the Land Veterans are not only beginning to recover from the drastic effects of post-traumatic stress disorder, but they are also demonstrating an alternative to industrial agriculture, which has its grip on this country. Pastor Emerson takes the idea "care for the land, it will take care of you" into the spiritual realm. She advocates that not only will the land help cure a troubled mind and a wounded body, but it also will nourish a person's soul.

At the risk of defying my father's and his father's advice to steer clear of religion, I will share these secular words of support for Pastor Emerson: "You go, girl." Pastor Emerson's upbeat and far-reaching goals for the Link Lake People's Church suffer from severe pushback in the Link Lake community. Some locals want no part of Pastor Emerson's "thin theology," as they refer to it. Of course, that is their right, and I will be the first to defend them.

But burning down a church building because someone doesn't believe in the church's theology goes many steps too far. And now, just last Sunday afternoon, another near tragedy occurred. With Pastor Emerson's congregation assembled in Oscar Anderson's barn, a culprit, perhaps the same one who burned down the church building in Link Lake, had a similar fate in mind for that big old red barn. To illustrate the depths of depravity to which some people will fall, the culprit shot and wounded Anderson's dog. We're told the dog is well on its way to recovery, but the Link Lake People's Church is still in shock over these two events.

Sheriff Jansen and several of his deputies continue to investigate both events. I'm told they've found some empty shell casings near the Anderson barn, which might provide a clue as to who is causing such mayhem in the Link Lake community. Let us hope that Sheriff Jansen will get to the bottom of all of this, and let us hope that the greater Link Lake community will begin to bring itself together, rather than finding new ways to split itself apart.

# 15

"So is your barn still standin'?" asked Fred Russo as he pulled up a chair opposite Oscar Anderson at their reserved table at the Eat Well.

"Yup, still is. But I'm worried," said Oscar as he glanced at the menu in front of him.

"How's your dog?"

"Rex is doin' okay. Still limps a little. I think it was Rex who saved my barn last Sunday."

"Think you're right," said Fred. "What in the hell is goin' on in our community, churches burnin', dogs bein' shot?"

"Wish I knew," said Oscar, beckoning to the waitress that he was ready to order. "Did get some good news yesterday. The community needs some good news."

"And what would that be?" asked Fred, who was sipping his freshly poured coffee.

"Pastor Vicki got a big surprise. A huge surprise. The Back to the Land Veterans raised about a thousand dollars toward a new church. Not a lot, but a start. Yesterday she got some more good news. Guess what? That notice she put on the internet resulted in some $750,000 dollars being donated. Image that: three-quarter million dollars from a message on the internet—which I don't use at all."

"Is she gonna build? Rumor has it that she's plannin' to leave Link Lake and find a new home for her church," said Fred.

"Where'd you hear that?"

"Saw John Wilson on the street the other day. As you probably know, John belongs to the Church of the Holy Redeemed. That church is no fan of Pastor Vicki's church and the Back to the Land Veterans. Don't know why he went off on me, other than I knew his dad pretty well. Anyway, he figured Pastor Vicki would be movin' and said it would be good riddance."

"Never did know what to make of John Wilson. I knew his dad too, decent, hardworkin' farmer. How he could raise a son like John, we'll never know. For the record, Pastor Vicki has no intention of leavin'. Since she's been livin' at my place she never once mentioned leavin'—she's all excited about buildin' a new church," said Oscar.

"With all those contributions, I suspect she'll start buildin' soon," said Fred.

"She's meetin' with an architect tomorrow, as a matter of fact."

"Sheriff got any leads on who burned the church and shot your dog?" asked Fred.

"Not a whisper. Whoever did it must be livin' around here, but who it is, and why would they wanna burn down a church, especially one like the Link Lake People's Church? Makes no sense," Oscar said, shaking his head.

Both men began working on the stacks of pancakes that had just appeared in front of them.

"What about this pipeline company that supposedly wants to lay pipe here in central Wisconsin?" asked Fred. "Any word?"

"Nary a peep out of them. You know, new pipelines aren't all that popular these days. Several arguments against them, especially pipelines that move crude oil from the tar pits in Alberta, Canada, to the refineries here in the states. I've been doin' a little reading. Fred, did you know that the crude oil comin' from Alberta is mined just like silver or gold is mined? The oil comes from open pits where the oil people dig for something called bitumen."

"I didn't know that. Doubt many people know that," said Fred. "So, where's the oil?"

"Well, best I can understand it, the folks workin' in what I'll call oil mines put together a concoction of water, clay, and sand, which releases the bitumen. This bitumen is further processed with some twelve barrels of bitumen, producing one barrel of crude oil," said Oscar, rather pleased with himself that at least at one level he understood something about the tar sands region and how oil is produced from it. "Of course, the process is tearin' up lots of the province of Alberta," said Oscar. "Beautiful forest land being torn to hell."

"Sounds complicated compared to pumpin' crude oil straight from the ground," said Fred, who had stopped eating to ponder what Oscar was sharing.

"Sounds complicated to me too. Of course, how the crude oil is produced has nothin' to do with the pipeline itself. Construction of a pipeline can also tear up lots of the landscape, to say nothin' about the possibility that the pipes leak and create an oil spill that can ruin farmland and pollute lakes and rivers," said Oscar.

"Jeez, Oscar, I hope that the pipeline doesn't consider Settlers Valley as a place it wants to cross. We don't need a crude oil pipeline for a neighbor," said Fred. "Reminds me of the sand mine that some people were pushin' a few years ago. That idea fell through—good thing, too."

"I hope the pipeline company either doesn't come at all or finds a place where it will do the least damage. These disabled vets surely don't need yet another blow to their recovery," said Oscar.

Fred took the last sip of his coffee. "Gotta go," he said. "Hey, you all set for the rhubarb festival? Dates are comin' up fast. May the best winemaker win." He clamped one of his big hands on Oscar's shoulder when he said it and smiled broadly.

# 16

On a warm May afternoon, ten veterans showed up for the second writers' workshop. Oscar was pleased. For those with commercial-sized vegetable gardens, this was planting time. Although both Oscar Anderson and Fred Russo helped the veterans with working up the soil and smoothing it in preparation for planting, the fields still had to be marked, and then each vegetable seed carefully and meticulously planted, following the directions for how deep and how far apart the seeds should be placed.

"Thanks for comin'," said Oscar as a way of greeting. "Nice day. I suspect most of you have work to do at home." He saw several heads nodding in the affirmative.

"How many of you took a stab at writin' in a journal since last we met?"

Every hand went up.

"Anybody comfortable in sharin' what you wrote?"

Ben Rostom's hand went up. "I'll give it a shot," he said.

"Thank you, Ben," said Oscar.

Ben began, "May 15, the temperature at 8 a.m., sixty degrees. Sky clear. Looks like another nice day. The three hundred chicks I got last month are really doing well. I have Fred Russo to especially thank for putting me onto this project. Fred even helped me build a couple little portable chicken houses that I can move with the old Farmall tractor I bought last year. By the way, Fred went with me to an auction where we got the old tractor for a song. Fred said those old tractors have a lot of life left if you take care of them. He showed me how to change the oil and replace the oil filter. I can't believe how generous Fred was with his time. I didn't know squat about chickens, chicken houses, or tractors when I rented these half-dozen acres. And look at me now: I'm a chicken farmer. But I better not brag. Fred says you never can learn enough about farming. Then he said something that I've been mulling over. Fred said in the business of farming, every year is the same and yet every year is different. You know, he's right about that. He really got me thinking. He said, each year we have winter and then spring arrives. But each spring is different from the one before it, and it will be different from next year's spring. That old Fred, he might look kind of plain and ordinary, but he's no dummy. You can bet your life on that."

"Ben, that's great. Very well done," said Oscar. Everyone clapped. Maggie Werch held up her hand. "I've got a short one," she said.

"May 16th, cloudy. The temperature at 7:00 a.m., fifty-eight degrees. I wish this old woodstove in my kitchen didn't have a mind of its own. I decided I would learn how to cook on it. It's not easy cooking on a woodstove. It's either not hot enough, or it's too hot. That is if I can get it going in the first place."

Everyone chuckled at Maggie's confession. Her fellow disabled veterans had come to know her as a no-nonsense woman who knew how to do just about everything.

"Any of you take a stab at writin' about a person who made a difference in your life?" asked Oscar.

Little Joey George, the smallest and the youngest of the group, held up his hand. He had taken to farming like a thirsty horse takes to water. Joey was not married, lived alone, and always had a smile on his face. Yet the group knew that underneath that veneer of happiness was a disabled veteran with a story that had changed his life.

Joey began. "Her name was Mable Cotsworth. She was my sixth-grade teacher. My fellow students all called her 'Mean Mable,' but not so she could hear of course. I thought she was about the meanest human being that ever walked the face of this good earth. If she ever wanted to become a drill sergeant, she would have been a good one. I hated her at the time because she was always on my case. Making sure I spelled words right. Making sure I finished all my math problems. She was even on me if I didn't sit up straight at my desk. But when I think about Miss Cotsworth today, I see nothing but a caring, loving woman who wanted me to get the best possible education. She never once put me down, but always challenged me to do better. She's dead now. Oh, how I wish I had taken time after I graduated from college to tell her what a difference she had made in my life. She knew me better than I knew me."

"Thank you, Joey," said Oscar. Several others in the group read pieces, and with each sharing, they appeared to be a little more comfortable in talking about personal things that they were at first reluctant to share. Oscar remembered how Pastor Vicki told him to not push these disabled veterans into telling their war stories. First get them comfortable with you and with one another. Oscar was pleased that already at this second session, several veterans who had not said a word at the first workshop had now begun to share some of their stories.

"Your assignment for next time," Oscar stated, looking out over the group, "is to write about some event that changed your life."

# 17

It had been boringly quiet for C.J. Anderson, who sat in the little office in the back of the BTTL Grocery Cooperative. Until the stranger walked in. It was C.J.'s afternoon to work at the office, and he didn't mind volunteering to do it. It was even kind of fun when he was busy answering phone calls and talking to people stopping by for a variety of reasons. But it was May, and all the BTTL veterans were busy planting. He wished he was home planting too, as it would be several more days before he had his three-acre plot planted to the variety of vegetables that he grew.

As he sat at the worn and scarred wooden desk—the group had purchased all the office furniture at a resale store in Willow River—he was thinking back to two years ago when he first moved to Settlers Valley and took up farming. How perceptive and thoughtful was his grandfather Oscar Anderson to recognize how much he was hurting both physically and mentally when he was discharged from the army. He was thankful to the folks at Walter Reed Hospital for all they had done so he could walk again with part of a leg that was not his but now had become so. When he was released from the hospital, he thought all would be well and that he could return to civilian life with no problems. He had not realized how much more healing he had needed. And how difficult it would be.

*Grandpa was right*, thought C.J. *The land can heal. It seems to be working for me.*

C.J. remembered how convincing his grandfather was when he offered these five acres of land to him, no strings attached. C.J. recalled how he had encouraged several of his military friends, all disabled in one way or another and whom he had met at Walter Reed, to join him here in Settlers Valley. Now, with the third growing season just around the corner, C.J. was reflecting on what he and his fellow veterans had accomplished.

He immediately thought how much more they would have struggled had Pastor Vicki not decided to come to Link Lake and organize a church. The church was the glue that held the disabled veterans together. Through good times and bad, the church was always there. But the church was no more, gone up in flames, destroyed by someone who didn't understand what the church was doing, or, perhaps more likely, despised what the church was doing.

C.J. was well aware that several vets were struggling with farming and adjusting to country living. He thought it had been one of his better ideas to ask both Fred Russo and his grandfather to serve as informal consultants to the new farmers. Most of the veterans had heard how industrial farming had taken over much of agriculture, with thousands of dairy cows in one barn, hundreds of hogs confined in one building, and thousands of acres of land growing the same crop year after year. If that was farming, they didn't want to do it, indeed couldn't do it, for none of them had the necessary resources to get started.

Oscar and Fred had retired from farming before large-scale farming had come along. They had learned from their fathers, who in turn had learned from their fathers, about farming and the necessity of treating the land as more than merely an economic asset. They had learned that if you take care of the land, it will take care of you. And they had earned a good living doing it.

With Oscar and Fred's help and equipment, the Back to the Land Veterans' farms were coming along nicely. And just this past winter, five new veteran families moved to the valley and joined the farming group. Farming wasn't easy, and most of the money the Back to the Land Veterans brought in from selling their produce went back into their farm operations. Thankfully, the veterans received disability pay, which helped them keep afloat financially as they became established as farmers.

Only one of the original group of vets that C.J. met at Walter Reed Hospital had given up farming in the valley and left. Randy Budwell lived alone and had tried to raise vegetables on his rented five acres, but his psychological wounds were so deep that apparently not even the land could help him. C.J. had stopped by Randy's farm several times, and what he witnessed was never twice the same. Some days Randy was busy working his land and he appeared happy. Other times he ranted about how the world was against him, the government was against him, and farming was a farce. After Randy left the valley unannounced more than a year ago, Pastor Vicki had done some checking and learned that he was a patient at the veterans hospital in Madison.

C.J., as he sat alone in the little BTTL office on Main Street, was pleased that he had been able to put to good use the skills and knowledge about farming that he had learned from his grandfather when he was a kid. He was also pleased that he was able to help some of his fellow disabled vets get started in farming. He thought, *What an unusual trio of farm consultants: a disabled army vet and two old retired farmers in their eighties.*

C.J. was thinking about Randy Budwell when a stranger opened the office door, entered, and removed his cap. C.J. didn't recall ever seeing him before. *Probably some newspaper reporter from out East or some TV producer wanting a story about the disabled vets living in the valley,* he thought. *Almost once a week one of these characters shows up. Looking for a story that is a little different. Realizing that many people are quite taken by the fate of disabled military veterans, and what some of them were doing with their lives.*

"You wouldn't happen to be C.J. Anderson?" the man asked. He had a quiet, firm way of speaking with a hint of a southern accent. C.J. had buddies in the military who talked just like this.

"Yes, I'm C.J. Anderson," said C.J., wondering what the fellow wanted.

"My name is Richard Barnes," the fellow said, extending his hand. "I'm from Houston, Texas, and I've talked with your grandpa Oscar. Everybody calls me Dick."

"You . . . you . . . you're Richard Barnes," stammered C.J. This was the man his grandfather had told him about—the one with the deep pockets and an interest in helping the vets farming in Settlers Valley.

Barnes laughed. "I suspect I pull on my pants the same way that you do."

"What can I do for you, Mr. Barnes?" asked C.J.

"First I want to tell you how inspired I am by what you're doin' for disabled veterans. My son, Josh, was in the service. He was killed in Iraq. A senseless war."

"I'm so sorry to hear that," said C.J. "Most of the vets living here fought in Afghanistan. I did three tours there myself."

"I don't know much about farmin', but from what I've read and what I hear is goin' on here, the land can be very healin'."

"That's what Grandpa believes. He told me that one of my distant relatives fought in the Civil War and came home in bad shape, both physically and mentally. He homesteaded the farm where Grandpa lives today."

"That's a great story, C.J.," Barnes said. He hesitated for a moment. "I've got an idea I'd like to run past y'all. But first, tell me how things are goin'. Let's see, this is the third year for your group, right?"

"Yup, third season is just coming up. Twenty disabled vet families live in Settlers Valley. Five new families arrived just this past winter," said C.J. "Some are doing better than others. Most knew nothing about farming, so it takes some time to learn," said C.J. "Several are married and have children. A few are single. I'm one of the not married." C.J smiled.

"To be honest with you, several are struggling," he continued. "It's hard earning a living growing a few acres of vegetables, some free-range chickens, or whatever enterprise interests them. And, we're getting some pushback. The Eagle Party doesn't understand what we're trying to do. They call us socialists and some even question our patriotism. Imagine questioning our patriotism after we all had fought for this country? Just gets up my hackles. And there's a church here in Link Lake, the Church of the Holy Redeemed, that believes that if we attend the Link Lake People's Church, we are all going straight to hell. Little hard to stomach that kind of hatred. But we are working at it."

Barnes listened carefully to what C.J. was saying. He hesitated for a moment, and then said, "Would it be possible for y'all to meet with me in the next day or so? I've got an idea I'd like to run up your flagpole."

"Yeah, that'd work. How do I get in touch with you? I'd like to invite Pastor Vicki Emerson to come too. She was an army chaplain and has been working with the vets here in the valley."

"Sure," said Barnes. "Bring her along." He shared his cell phone number.

# 18

The next day, at one thirty, Richard Barnes, Pastor Vicki, and C.J. Anderson sat at a table in a quiet corner of the Eat Well Café, each with a fresh cup of coffee.

"I'm pleased to meet you," Barnes said to Pastor Vicki. "I can't say enough how impressed I am with the vets farmin' here in Settlers Valley. I understand that y'all have been helpin' them."

"Well, thank you," Pastor Vicki said. "Appreciate it."

"I heard about what happened to your church. I just can't imagine someone would do somethin' like that," said Barnes.

"That's not all," said C.J. "When the congregation was meeting in Grandpa's barn a couple of Sundays ago, somebody tried the same thing. Grandpa's dog got to him first."

"They arrest anyone?" Barnes asked.

"Not yet. Sheriff's working on it," said C.J.

"Most people support what we're doing here," said Pastor Vicki. "Our fund drive on the internet brought in $750,000 from people all across the country. These folks want to help us build a new Link Lake People's Church. Some terrific people in this world." She brushed a tear from her eye.

"Yes, there are," said Barnes. "Y'all are plannin' on rebuildin', aren't you? I overheard somebody say that you might be packin' it up and movin' on."

"Don't know how that rumor got started—probably from somebody who wishes we'd leave. Somebody who doesn't like what our church stands for. Lots of hate around here these days. Lots of blaming. Lots of rumors."

C.J. was nodding in agreement.

"I'd planned to build even before the donations started coming in. I'm not going anywhere. Link Lake People's Church isn't either." Pastor Vicki said it with force and conviction. C.J. was smiling. "I don't want to sound arrogant or like a know-it-all," she said, "but this community needs our church."

"Sounds like you're speakin' the truth, pastor," said Barnes.

"Just call me Vicki," she said.

"Well," Barnes began, "y'all are probably wondering what brought me all the way from Houston to little Link Lake, Wisconsin."

"Just wondering a little," C.J. said, smiling.

"Well, I represent the Herman Barnes Family Foundation. Our offices are in Houston, Texas. We're not very big—my grandfather started the foundation fifty years ago when he came into some money. What we do is give grants to worthy causes—and I'm convinced that your Back to the Land Veterans group certainly qualifies," Barnes said.

"Interesting," was all that C.J. could think to say. He pulled a bit on his beard, something he did when he faced something new.

"Ready for refills?" interrupted the waitress with a big smile. "The first cup you pay for, but after that it's free."

Barnes continued, "When your grandpa mentioned that Settlers Valley was settled by Civil War veterans usin' the federal government's 1862 Homestead Law, it got me thinkin'. That law made thousands of acres of federal land available to farmers who essentially got their land free. I studied up on the law a little." Barnes dug into his pocket for a sheet of paper that he unfolded and began reading: "The 1862 Homestead Act offered a grant of 160 acres of public land to any adult citizen, or someone intendin' to become a citizen, who headed a family and who had never borne arms against the U.S. government. The only payment was a modest registration fee. The person receivin' the grant was required to build a dwellin' and cultivate the land."

"I remember my grandpa telling me about the Homestead Act," said C.J. He now wondered where Barnes was headed and what an 1862 law had to do with today and a bunch of disabled veterans.

"Here's my idea," said Barnes as he folded the paper and put it back in his pocket. "I'd like to start a mini homestead program for disabled veterans right here. Right here in Settlers Valley." Barnes made a sweeping motion with his arm.

"I'm listening," said Pastor Vicki.

"What if our foundation provided enough money so veterans could own up to ten acres of land? If they built a home and cultivated the land for five years, the land would be theirs, free and clear," said Barnes.

"I don't quite get how it would work." said C.J., wrinkling his brow.

"Here's what I've figured out. An idea for y'all to consider. Pastor Vicki would establish a disabled veterans' homestead fund at her church. Our foundation would provide the money. I'd like to call it the Josh Barnes Memorial Homestead Fund, in memory of my son. C.J., you and Vicki would review applications and approve those to receive homestead money, with the help of an elected committee of local farmers already livin' in the valley." Barnes paused and then added, "Of course our lawyers would take care of all the legal details for the program."

"You would do that?" asked Vicki. "I know that all of the vets are renting their property, with rent-to-buy agreements. C.J. already owns his five acres, a gift from his grandfather."

"It's the least I can do. Rather than 160 acres, I'd make the limit ten acres, to be in tune with your concept of small-acreage farmin'. It would work this way: the foundation would provide funds so vets could buy the land they are now rentin'. The money would be granted them with provisions similar to the 1862 Homestead Law. Like with the original law, if they left their land before livin' on it for five years, or fail to make improvements, they'd have to return the money."

"That is most generous of you, Mr. Barnes," said Vicki.

"It's Dick, Vicki. Just call me Dick."

C.J. thrust out his hand to shake Barnes's. "You are incredibly generous. When could all of this begin?"

"Within a few days, I'll have our attorneys draft up a model contract. When we have the contracts ready, the vets here in Settlers Valley can apply and we'll go from there," said Barnes.

After the last sips of coffee and another round of handshakes, Barnes took his leave. C.J. and Vicki could not contain the joy they felt as they left the Eat Well on this sunny day in May.

"Our Back to the Land Veterans just got the boost they needed," said C.J.

"It would seem so," said Pastor Vicki. "It would seem so."

# 19

Sheriff Jansen was more than a little concerned when he learned about the elaborate Memorial Day celebration that the Back to the Land Veterans had planned. Jansen drove out to C.J. Anderson's place as soon as he heard about the plans for a parade.

"This will be the biggest parade ever held in Link Lake," C.J. said when the sheriff asked if they could talk about the Memorial Day plans.

"I don't know how to tell you this, but I wish you wouldn't do the parade. I don't know if I have enough deputies to protect you and your fellow vets," the sheriff said. "Link Lake got rid of its police department a couple of years ago, as you probably know, and turned its policing over to us. Other small communities are doing that too. A way to save money," the sheriff added.

"You know what, Sheriff, I think the vets who will be in the parade know how to take care of themselves. They've all faced danger and know how to spot it too," said C.J.

"C.J., there'll be lots of folks in the parade who do not have the experience the vets have had: 4-H members, band participants, volunteer firefighters, church members. All of these folks will be in danger, to say nothing about the people who'll be lining Main Street watching the parade," said the sheriff. He continued, "Somebody or a group of somebodies are out to get you and your veterans' group. They are sick people, that's for sure. Look what happened to your church. Burned to the ground. Look what happened when church services were held in your grandfather's barn. Gunfire and your grandpa's dog shot. I'm worried about Memorial Day. It would be the perfect time for these dangerous people to do something worse, even a mass killing of people. It's happened in other parts of the country, as you know."

"Sheriff, I appreciate your concern. I really do. But I think we'll be okay. The vets here in Settlers Valley are really looking forward to Memorial Day and this parade. After all, isn't Memorial Day a time for applauding the military veterans?" said C.J.

"You are so right, C.J., but it's my job to help keep people in Ames County safe," said the sheriff.

"I know that." Changing the subject, C.J. asked, "Any leads on who burned down the church and shot Grandpa's dog?"

"We don't know a whole lot," said the sheriff. "We found shell casings near where your grandpa's dog was shot and some blood spattered on the ground. We sent that evidence to the crime lab in Madison. But so far I've not gotten back any word."

"Have you met Maggie Werch, Sheriff?"

"I have not. Who is she?"

"Maggie moved onto one of the small acreage farms this past winter. Like a lot of other vets in Settlement Valley, she's suffering from PTSD. It's a terrible problem for most vets, I must admit, for me included. But what I wanted to tell you is this. Maggie was a military police officer in the army. She worked as a military crime investigator. I haven't mentioned this to Maggie, but if you wouldn't object, I believe Maggie might be of some help in figuring out the identity of these criminals."

"Sure, I'd welcome her ideas," the sheriff said. "I'll talk to her. Maybe she can help us get off dead center in figuring out who is causing all this trouble."

"See you at the parade," C.J. said as the sheriff climbed into his police cruiser and drove away.

C.J. sat on the porch of his cabin, his dog, Lucky, by his side.

"Well, Lucky," C.J. said. "At least the sheriff is on our side and wants to help. With the way things are going here in Link Lake, we need all the help we can get."

Lucky began wagging his tail.

"Do you know what some folks in Link Lake call us vets? They call us a bunch of crippled soldiers with wild ideas about farming. Imagine that? I'm a crippled soldier with wild ideas. Imagine that, Lucky?"

The big dog put its muzzle on C.J.'s knee.

"What do you think? I don't like to be called crippled—disabled would be better—but I kinda like being tagged for having wild ideas about farming. Maybe some of us vets are the future of what farming might be."

Sheriff Jansen wasn't the only one concerned about what might happen on Memorial Day. Pastor Vicki was near sick with worry. She knew that the followers of the Church of the Holy Redeemed were dead set against the Link Lake People's Church, the pastor going so far as to call Pastor Vicki the Antichrist, a tool of the devil. Chilling words. She had even heard someone in Link Lake refer to the People's Church as the "Crippled Vets' Church." She saw the parade as a way to help the community realize that veterans lived in their midst, and to show them that they should honor what the veterans have done to keep this country safe and to protect the many freedoms that they often take for granted.

Pastor Vicki served on the town's Memorial Day committee, along with school principal Lucy James and Bill Baxter, editor of the *Ames County Argus*. It had been relatively easy to put the parade together. Everyone they asked replied, "Yes, we'd be happy to be a part of it." All except Pastor Jacob John Jacob of the Church of the Holy Redeemed. His reply to committee chair Lucy James, after she had told him that the Link Lake People's Church would have a float in the parade, was: "Under no circumstances will we be in any event where the Link Lake People's Church will be featured. That church is a menace to every God-fearing citizen in the Link Lake community and their pastor is a fraud." Lucy shared the response with Pastor Vicki. Pastor Jacob's tirade only increased Pastor Vicki's concern that something awful might happen during the parade.

Memorial Day dawned with a clear sky, no prediction of rain, and temperatures to climb into the low seventies by parade time, which was scheduled for ten. Starting at nine, the various entries in the parade began organizing on the Link Lake school athletic field. Pastor Vicki, helping with the organization of the parade, saw two sheriff's deputy patrol cars sitting next to the athletic field, one on either side. Two deputies stood by each vehicle. She saw that they were holding assault weapons. Pastor Vicki had asked one of the patrol cars to lead the parade and the second one to be the last vehicle in the parade. Sheriff Jansen had assured her that he would also have several well-armed plainclothes deputies in the audience. If anything, the deputies reinforced Pastor Vicki's fears as real, as the sheriff, too, was expecting something terrible to happen during the parade.

Promptly at 10:00 a.m., a sheriff's car, with lights flashing, led off the parade. A short distance behind marched the Link Lake High School band, playing a John Philip Sousa tune. Next came the disabled veterans, most marching but four of them riding on a hay wagon brightly decorated with red, white, and blue streamers. Oscar Anderson's old Farmall tractor, with Oscar driving, pulled the wagon.

The Link Lake 4-H Club members followed. Then came the first of five fire trucks, the first one from the Link Lake Volunteer Fire Department, followed by a beautiful float representing the Link Lake People's Church. The Willow River High School band came next, then the Willow River Fire Department's bright-red truck, with all lights flashing.

C.J. had been right. This was the biggest parade that Link Lake had ever witnessed. Nearly a half hour had passed before the second deputy's car brought up the rear, with all lights flashing and an occasional blast of its siren.

The sheriff had been wrong. Pastor Vicki had been wrong. The parade came off without a hitch. No disturbances, no gunfire, just the sweet music of marching bands and the cheering of little children and their parents lining the parade route.

C.J. saw Pastor Vicki back at the school athletic field. Both were smiling.

"No problems, except that Grandpa's tractor ran out of gas about two-thirds of the way along the parade route and the ablest of the vets plus several husky bystanders pushed the tractor and wagon to the side to let the rest of the parade pass by," said C.J.

"I'm thrilled," said Pastor Vicki.

"Maybe whoever was causing us all this trouble has given up," said C.J.

"I hope so."

# 20

Settlers Valley was abuzz with activity, as the spring weather provided needed showers and increasingly warmer and sunny days. Veterans busily planted vegetables while they enjoyed the warm weather after a long winter. In early June, everyone was looking forward to the annual rhubarb festival, which previously was headquartered in the community room of the Link Lake People's Church. With the community room a pile of ashes, the festival moved to the Anderson farm.

With much of their planting completed, the vets looked forward to the festival. The festivities began on Friday evening with a dance that started at nine. The results of the rhubarb pie and wine contests would be announced just before the closing down of the event at six o'clock on Saturday.

By quarter past eight Friday evening, guests began arriving. The two big barn doors, the entryway to the barn's vast haylofts, were pushed open, allowing the breeze onto what tonight would be a dance floor. C.J. stood at the entrance, greeting everyone who arrived for the dance.

He was pleased to see Maggie Werch walking up the ramp to the open doors. She wore a big smile and a beautiful black dress. When he had visited her little farm a few weeks earlier, she was wearing a red-and-black-checkered flannel shirt and baggy bib overalls— entirely appropriate for working in her fields. For a moment, C.J.

was so taken by this "other Maggie," he stood speechless. Maggie walked up to him and touched his arm with her hand.

"Hi, C.J.," she said, continuing to smile. "It's been a long time since I've been to a dance. Been nearly as long since I've worn this dress. Am I overdressed?" she whispered as she looked around and saw lots of blue jeans and flannel shirts.

"No, no," blurted out C.J. "You are . . . you are . . ." He wanted to say "so beautiful," but he hesitated. "You . . . you are here," he stupidly said.

"Well, yes, I clearly am," Maggie said. "Will you save a dance for me? I've heard you are part of the band, but they won't miss you for one dance."

"Yes, yes, I'll do that," said C.J. He caught the subtle smell of lilac. It was Maggie's perfume.

"One more thing. Could you stop out to the farm next week on Wednesday? I have some questions. I'll fix lunch," Maggie said.

"Sure," said C.J.

By eight thirty, the Anderson barn was filled with people, everyone looking forward to the opening event of the rhubarb festival, which was always a surprise to the crowd. Last year the inaugural event had featured students from the Link Lake Middle School choir.

Pastor Vicki, emcee of the event this year, took the microphone. "Welcome to our annual rhubarb festival. Before I introduce our special opening event, let me say a word or two about what's planned for this year's festival. Tonight the Settlers Valley Ramblers will offer their musical talents for dancing. What better way to celebrate rhubarb than a good old foot-stomping dance! Tomorrow morning, starting at 7:00 a.m., we'll have our annual Rhubarb Run, this year from Link Lake to the Anderson farm. You probably noticed when you arrived here this evening that we have booths representing many organizations. We also have food tents featuring all things rhubarb: rhubarb cake, rhubarb crisp, rhubarb pie, and—of course, how can I forget—rhubarb wine. Judging of the rhubarb pie and rhubarb wine contest entries will take place tomorrow afternoon. We'll announce the winners at our closing ceremony at 6:00 p.m. But now our special opening event. Let's have a big round of applause for Oscar Anderson, who has penned an Ode to Rhubarb. Oscar, you are on."

Wearing his best pair of bib overalls and a bright-red shirt, Oscar took the microphone. When the clapping ceased, he began.

"First, let me say welcome to my farm. I'm proud to have the event headquarters here this year. Some folks said we should cancel the festival after the community room at the church burned. But what would spring be like without our rhubarb festival?"

Loud clapping and even a couple of whistles.

Oscar cleared his throat and began:

*Ode to Rhubarb*
Oh, Rhubarb, Rhubarb,
With your fresh stalk thumbing winter,
As you push forth new growth almost at
The same time that the last snow of winter shrivels and
    disappears.
Oh, Rhubarb, brave Rhubarb
With your beautiful green leaves
And bright red stalks.
With a history that goes back thousands of years
To China, where the Rhubarb root was medicine
Strong medicine.
Medicine for stomach ailments,
As an enhancer of appetite,
Oh, Rhubarb, beautiful Rhubarb
Today we enjoy pie, cake, sauce,
And even some wine.

All made from the Rhubarb stalk.
Oh, Rhubarb, beautiful Rhubarb,
We applaud you.
For just being Rhubarb.


Oscar handed the microphone back to Pastor Vicki and sat down as the crowd applauded. "Thank you, Oscar, for those thoughtful words about rhubarb. But now, it's time for celebration. It's time to celebrate rhubarb. Here are the Settlers Valley Ramblers!"

Pastor Vicki picked up the guitar that was leaning against the barn wall and joined the other three members of the band, who were already tuning up: C.J. Anderson on the trumpet, Sheriff Jansen on the accordion, and school principal Lucy James on the keyboard.

Dancers immediately filled the dance floor where once bales of hay had been stacked. They danced polkas, old-time waltzes, circle two-steps, and schottisches. They laughed and clapped and danced some more. While the band played the "Tennessee Waltz," C.J. put down his trumpet and danced with Maggie, who snuggled up close to him. C.J. couldn't remember the last time he had been this close to a good-looking woman. And oh, how she could dance.

With the song over, C.J. said, "Got to get back to my trumpet. Thanks for the dance."

"See you next Wednesday," Maggie said, smiling.

The dance had been going on for more than an hour when a massive "kaboom" echoed across the barn floor. Almost immediately all the lights went out, and the old barn became as dark as a cave on a Halloween night. Everyone stopped in place, believing that the lights would come back on. But not Sheriff Jansen, who quickly fished a small flashlight from one of his pockets and felt for his pistol in a holster attached to his belt, and under his shirt, so it was invisible. On the other side of his belt, the sheriff reached for his radio.

"What's goin' on out there?" shouted the sheriff into his radio. He had a half-dozen plainclothes deputies working both outside and inside the barn.

The sheriff rushed to the big double doors. The only sound was the loud barking of Oscar's big collie dog, tied up on Oscar's porch. A full moon was edging up over the horizon, providing a bit of light for what had been a very black night.

"Over here, Sheriff," one of the deputies said into the radio. "By the pump house." The sheriff hurried to where the deputy had directed.

"What've you got?" asked Jansen.

"Looks like somebody lit one of them aerial bombs that fireworks guys set off on the Fourth of July," the deputy said, pointing at remnants of charred paper on the ground.

"That would account for the loud boom," the sheriff said. "Where's Oscar Anderson? He'd know where the electric switch box is for the barn."

"Here I am," said Oscar as he hurried toward the pump house. "The switch box is in the pump house, on the wall just beyond the pump."

Using his flashlight, the sheriff spotted the fuse box. The door was open. He quickly noticed that all of the switches had been tripped. One after the other the sheriff pushed the switches back to on, and once more the lights came on in the barn and all over the farmstead.

But the dance was over. People were heading for their cars, a bit shaken by what had happened and in too much of a hurry to find out the cause before leaving the Anderson farm. Whoever had set off the aerial bomb and turned out all the lights had gotten what he wanted. He wanted to create fear.

The next day the early morning Rhubarb Run brought out only half as many as had run the race the previous year. And festival attendance during the day was down 40 percent from last year. Nobody wanted to say it out loud, but they were afraid. What would be next?

The rhubarb pie and wine contest went on as planned, but no more than twenty-five people showed up at the Anderson barn to hear who won this year's contests. Both Oscar Anderson and Fred Russo were there of course, but to their surprise, first place for rhubarb wine went to Gertrude Eldermost, who lived on the other side of Link Lake. Gertrude won the rhubarb pie contest as well. A double winner.

# 21

The following Wednesday, C.J. worked a couple of hours in his garden and then returned to his cabin, took a shower, and trimmed his beard. Lucky stood watching and wondering what was going on as his master never showered twice in one morning, and almost never trimmed his beard. C.J. then pulled on a clean shirt and clean blue jeans before climbing into his pickup and, along with Lucky, drove the two miles to Maggie's farm. He thought about how he had shown her how to light a wood-burning cookstove and wondered what questions she had for him today. "Did she know how to use a garden hoe?" he chuckled to himself.

June, with all the oaks, the aspens, the maples leafed out, and the pastures greening up and the sky blue with a few fluffy clouds skittering by, reminded C.J. some of what kept him in Settlers Valley. One of the fringe benefits of living in the valley was the beauty of it all, a beauty that changed as the seasons changed.

But C.J. wasn't thinking about the beauty of the day, or the little pigs he saw out on pasture, being raised by one of his fellow disabled vets, or the chickens that were in the field at another vet's farm. All he could think about on this beautiful spring day was the beautiful woman he had seen at the dance on Saturday night. He remembered military police officers as big, hard-nosed guys who took no guff from anyone, no matter if the rule the soldier broke was large or small. He never thought of any them as being beautiful women.

C.J. parked his pickup near the kitchen door of the old farmhouse where Maggie lived. With these warm days and nights, she didn't have to worry about starting the fire in the wood-burning cookstove to warm the place.

C.J. climbed out of his pickup and glanced at his watch; it was precisely eleven, the time she said he should arrive. He and Lucky walked up to the kitchen porch, and C.J. knocked on the kitchen door. He knew better than to knock on the front door of the old house. C.J. learned from his grandfather that farm folks seldom used the front door for entering their homes.

"You are right on time," said Maggie as she opened the door. Today she was wearing a blue-and-white-checkered shirt and blue jeans. Her blonde hair was down, touching her shoulders, and her blue eyes sparkled. C.J. said, "You're looking very farm-like on this sunny day." He thought, *This is the most beautiful woman I have ever seen.*

"Would you like to see my garden?" Maggie asked. "I think it's doing well, but I'd like your opinion."

"Sure," said C.J. "But first I have some good news for you and all the disabled vets here in Settlers Valley."

"Good news?" asked Maggie.

"I've just learned that you and your fellow members of the Back to the Land Veterans who are in rent-to-buy agreements can apply for a grant, with no strings attached, to get enough money to buy your land. All of the vets are renting with the right to purchase except me." C.J. went on to explain the details of the Josh Barnes Memorial Homestead Fund.

"Wow, that's good news," Maggie said. "Who's providing the money?"

"The Herman Barnes Family Foundation. A guy by the name of Richard Barnes is associated with the foundation. He heard about the Back to the Land Veterans and decided to do something to honor his son, Josh, who was in the army and died in Iraq."

"When can I apply?"

"Soon," said C.J. He explained how the fund would be managed by the church and said the details for applying would be available in a week or so.

"Wonderful," was all Maggie could think to say. "But this sounds a bit too good to be true."

"I thought about that too," said C.J. "But I met with this Barnes fellow and he seems to be a straight shooter. Some of your fellow vets have been struggling to earn enough money—the Herman Barnes Family Foundation's generosity will surely make things easier."

"That's just great. I've always dreamed of owning some land. Barnes sure has his heart in the right place," said Maggie. "Oh," she continued, "Do you want to see what I've been doing?" She grabbed a jaunty little straw hat and pointed the way to one of her several vegetable plots, the first of which was a less than hundred yards from the farmstead.

"This is my tomato plot," Maggie said. "Remember when you showed me how to sow the tomato seeds in the little germination pots? Well, here they are, on their own. I've set out about two hundred of them."

"Looking good," C.J. said. "Before you know it, you'll have to stake them, so they don't fall over."

"You'll show me how?" Maggie said as she looked at C.J.

"Sure, I'll show you how." But it was evident that C.J., on this beautiful, warm June morning, was more interested in Maggie than her tomato plants.

C.J., Lucky, and Maggie walked on to inspect her potato field. She had planted about a half acre of potatoes, about one-third red potatoes and the remainder white ones. They checked the long rows of broccoli ready for a first cutting and several rows of radishes as well as rows of leaf lettuce of multiple colors ranging from deep green to deep purple. Maggie showed C.J. five long rows of carrots and as many rows of onions—all growing well and awaiting harvest in a few weeks.

"As you suggested, I didn't plant the vining crops—my cucumbers, squash, and pumpkins—until after Memorial Day. So they are just peeking through the ground." She had planted nearly a half acre of pumpkins, hoping for good sales during the fall harvest season.

She showed C.J. another garden plot. "I've planted this entire plot, you said it was a half acre, as I recall, with sweet corn. It's up and seems to be growing well, except for this little corner. There are tracks here, and something has been nibbling on the sweet corn. Look, these little corn plants are eaten right to the ground."

"Deer tracks," said C.J. "You've got a deer feasting on your corn. You're lucky it's only your corn. Deer love vegetable gardens. They'll eat just about anything you want to grow."

"I haven't seen any deer."

"They mostly eat just before it gets dark," said C.J.

"What do I do, make a scarecrow?" asked Maggie.

C.J. laughed. "Doubt a scarecrow would make much difference."

"So what do I do?"

"Well, Farmer Maggie, here's what I do to keep deer away from my garden crops." He went on to explain how he pounded removable metal posts around the garden about ten to fifteen feet apart, fastened insulators to each post, and then strung two wires all the way around his gardens. The wires were connected to a solar-powered electric fencing unit.

"But I don't want to hurt the deer even if they are chewing on my garden," said Maggie, looking skeptical.

"The fence really doesn't hurt the deer. When one of them touches the wire, it gets a slight shock, enough to remind the deer that she should eat elsewhere. I don't see any wild turkey tracks in your garden, but the wires will keep the turkeys away as well."

"Really? There are wild turkeys here too?" asked Maggie.

"There surely are, quite a bunch of them, and they and the deer can ruin a garden in no time at all," said C.J.

"You'll help me buy what I need for a fence?" asked Maggie.

"Sure will, I'll even help you put it up. Not too hard to do."

"Well, that's what I've been doing," Maggie said. "What do you think?"

"I think you are going to make a pretty darn good gardener," said C.J. "Of course beyond the hungry critters, you can count on weeds that want to crowd out your crops. Hoeing is part of the answer. And you'll need a rototiller as well. I think I know where you can get a used one."

Maggie sighed. "I know that, but I've got to fess up and say that so far my hoe and I are not really friends. And I trust you'll show me how to use a rototiller."

C.J. laughed. "That hoe and you will learn to get along—in fact, for a gardener, a hoe can be your best friend. You'll probably discover that you'll spend more time with your hoe than any friend—especially during June and July. You'll like running a rototiller too."

"Are you hungry?" asked Maggie, moving the conversation away from garden hoes and hoeing.

"I am," said C.J.

The two gardeners made their way back to the old, faded farmhouse. Lucky found himself right at home on a rug on the porch, while C.J. followed Maggie into the kitchen, where she had set two places at the table. She said, "The bathroom's just down the hall if you want to wash up before we eat."

When C.J. returned, he saw a huge bowl of salad in the middle of the table and a bottle of wine. "How about a glass of wine before we eat?" offered Maggie.

"Can't do it," said C.J. He wanted to explain why to Maggie but didn't believe this was the time to do it.

"Sorry," Maggie said. "How about a glass of cranberry juice?"

"That would be great," said C.J.

Maggie returned to the table with a container of cranberry juice and poured a glass for him and one for herself and said, "Have a seat. I put together this salad. The lettuce is from my garden, as are the radishes. The chicken I got from Ben Rostom. You can't beat the taste of free-range chicken. You know Ben of course."

"Yup, I know Ben. Infantry. He has two purple hearts."

"Here's a toast," Maggie said, lifting her glass of cranberry juice. "To a summer of ample rains and warm temps, fewer weeds, and deer and turkeys that will eat some other place than at my farm."

"Cheers," said C.J. as they clinked their glasses.

As the two young war veterans sat enjoying their lunch, they chatted about their pasts. Maggie shared a bit about what it was like growing up in Chicago and spending a couple of weeks each summer at Silver Lake just east of Link Lake. C.J. talked about summers on his grandfather's farm, where he had learned much more than he thought he was learning about how to farm, the importance of the land, and the value of neighbors. They talked about some of their fellow disabled veterans and how they were doing. C.J. mentioned Randy Budwell.

"The farm didn't work out for Randy. I tried to help him, and some days he seemed to be catching on. And other days when I was there, all I saw was an angry young man. He left without telling anybody why he was leaving, or where he was going. Pastor Vicki did a little checking and learned he is in the vets hospital in Madison," said C.J.

"I'm so sorry to hear that," said Maggie.

"Nobody is sorrier than I am. I guess I was a little more confident than I should have been that every disabled veteran could benefit from farming. I still believe that the land can help heal most of them—I see it every day all across Settlers Valley. I see it in myself. But Randy's case brought me back to reality. Not everyone heals in the same way."

After a few moments of silence, Maggie said, "I've got some news, C.J., thanks to you."

"News?" asked C.J.

"Sheriff Jansen stopped out here the other day."

"The sheriff stopped out here—what in the world did you do wrong?"

Maggie laughed. "He came out to see me based on your recommendation."

"My recommendation?"

"He wanted to talk with me about my military police experience, especially my work as a criminal investigator in the army. And you know what?" said Maggie.

"What?"

"He hired me as a part-time consultant in the sheriff's office, to help him from time to time. He even gave me a badge and an ID pack."

"Jeez, now I'll have to be careful what I do," said C.J.

"I don't think so," said Maggie quietly.

With their lunch finished, Maggie asked, "How about another glass of cranberry juice?"

"Sure," said C.J.

The young couple continued chatting for an hour, mostly about the future of the vets in Settlers Valley.

"Well, I better be going. Got lots of work to do at home," said C.J. "Thanks for the tour, and the great lunch. Anytime you have a question or need some help, give me a call."

When C.J. and Lucky were driving home, C.J.'s mind was awash with new thoughts and feelings, all of them centered on a former MP—Maggie Werch—his neighbor, a sheriff's office consultant, and a fellow disabled veteran who had taken up farming in Settlers Valley. But now, after but one lunch, Maggie Werch was much more than all of these things.

# 22

*Ames County Argus*
MISCHIEF AT RHUBARB FESTIVAL CUTS ATTENDANCE

Link Lake's rhubarb festival's attendance this year was about half compared to previous years. What Sheriff Jansen described as "malicious mischief" dramatically reduced the numbers. The sheriff said, "Somebody set off an aerial fireworks bomb and then cut the lights during the rhubarb festival's annual dance, this year held at Oscar Anderson's barn in Settlers Valley. In a panic, people left the dance, not aware that they weren't in any real danger."

This is the third such occurrence in the Link Lake community since this past April, when the Link Lake People's Church was destroyed by fire. The second was the fracas at the church service in Anderson's barn during which his dog was wounded by gunshot.

Sheriff Jansen asks that anyone who knows anything about these deeds contact his office. "These illegal activities have created a fear in the Link Lake residents, especially among the veterans living in Settlers Valley, the likes of which I have not seen in twenty years as a law enforcement officer. These young men and women have taken up small-acreage farming here to escape from the horrors of war and its associated side effects, only to see a new kind of hatred here in their own backyards," said Sheriff Jansen.

"You see the piece in the *Argus* about the festival?" asked Fred at their regular weekly coffee meeting at the Eat Well.

"I did," said Oscar. "I don't need to be reminded of what happened in my barn during the dance. People were scared to death when they heard that loud explosion—sounded like a bomb had gone off, and then when the lights went out, I could just feel the fear in the room. Believe me, I was one of those who was scared—weren't you, Fred?"

"I can't remember the last time the hair stood up on the back of my neck, and my knees began knockin'," Fred replied. "You had a barn full of people. What if some jerk had come in there with one of them automatic war weapons and killed a bunch of folks? Happens, Oscar. Happens all too often. You bet I was scared."

"I just don't know what this country is comin' to. Everybody is mad at somebody, it seems. So much hatred," said Oscar.

A huge stack of pancakes appeared in front of each of them. Oscar poured the syrup first. "Hey, save some for me," said Fred, smiling.

"Jeez, Fred, when did I ever use up all the syrup? Tell me that?"

Later, with their pancakes nearly gone, Oscar said, "There is something good to talk about this morning. C.J. told me about it. Remember that guy—Richard Barnes from Houston, Texas—that I talked to a few weeks back?"

"Yup, I remember. You were worried at the time that he might not be who he said he was and might be plannin' some scam against the vets here in Settlers Valley," said Fred.

"Well, Fred, not only is he for real, but he has done something that is beyond anything anyone would have expected," said Oscar, taking a long sip of coffee.

"What's he done?" asked Fred. Oscar went on to explain the details of the money Barnes would provide for the veterans in Settlers

99

Valley to purchase their small-acreage farms using funds from the Josh Barnes Memorial Homestead Fund.

"Funny thing is," Oscar said, "Barnes got the idea for this homestead fund from the 1862 U.S. Homestead Act, the same law that our ancestors used when they first came to Settlers Valley after the Civil War."

"How about that?" said Fred. "Here we are, more than 150 years later, and we see a bit of history repeating itself."

"You could say that," said Oscar.

"Weren't you listening? I did say that," said a smiling Fred.

"You know as well as I do that these vets' financial situations are a bit shaky. They get some disability pay from the government, but that's only enough to survive. And their farms are doin' pretty well, but they're not big moneymakers, not by a longshot. This new version of a homestead law just might make the difference for some of these vets to stay or leave."

"I have to agree with you, Oscar. Much as I dislike doin' it." Fred smiled.

"I think we can all relax a little, now that the church is being rebuilt, and the disabled vets have some financial insurance."

"I'm not one to be nosey, nor do I want to start any rumors, but I've noticed C.J.'s pickup parked at Maggie Werch's farm almost every day."

"Yeah, C.J. tells me she needs lots of help with her farmin' operations. C.J.'s been helpin' her. That's what he tells me anyway."

"I've yet to see the two of them outside," said Fred, grinning from ear to ear.

"Maybe somethin's going on beyond gardenin'," said Oscar. "Would be a good thing. C.J.'s been pretty wrapped up in gettin' this Back to the Land Veterans group off the ground, so to speak. And he's still fightin' that PTSD thing. Maybe he's found a little love in his life. I'll probably be the last to know." Oscar was smiling as he said it.

"That's something else that may help C.J.'s healin'," said Fred, chuckling.

# 23

The spring weather had been kind to the veteran farmers living in Settlers Valley. The rains had come, regularly, just enough, not too much, not too little. Rare. Too often a spring in central Wisconsin is either too wet and the farmers have trouble getting in their crops, or too dry and the seeds don't germinate well. But not this year. Even on the sandy and droughty soils in the valley, everything was growing rapidly. The only complaints that C.J. heard from his fellow small-acreage farmers could be summarized in one word: weeds. Too many weeds. Big weeds, little weeds. Ragweeds, quack grass, pigweeds, lamb's-quarter, thistles. Weeds between the rows. Weeds within the rows. One rule that the Back to the Land farmers had agreed to was not to use any chemical control of weeds. And they didn't. But the rototillers and garden hoes were surely getting a workout.

C.J. felt better each day. He was even sleeping better with no horrible nightmares. Once his close friend, Jack Daniels remained on the shelf as it had for nearly a year. He had not touched a drop of it.

His garden crops were looking the best they had since he had taken up farming in the valley. He also discovered he couldn't take his mind off the former military police officer who farmed only a short drive down the country road from his place and was also working part-time as a consultant in the sheriff's office. He and Maggie spent hours talking about their military adventures, about their growing up years, and recently about their future. Maggie had brought it up. "Do you ever think about getting married?" she asked one morning after C.J. had spent the night. She was making breakfast for him of eggs and bacon, prepared on the old woodstove that Maggie had now mastered. Lucky ate from his bowl that C.J. left at Maggie's place. The question was not one that C.J. had expected.

"I . . . I haven't thought much about it," mumbled C.J.

"Just wondering," said Maggie. "Just wondering."

The following Saturday, on what would become a warm June day, C.J., with Lucky, loaded the back of his pickup with a couple dozen quarts of strawberries, a half bushel of radishes washed but with the tops still on, several bunches of rhubarb, even more bunches of freshly cut asparagus, nearly a bushel of broccoli, and a half bushel of leaf lettuce that he had cut at daybreak.

By 7:00 a.m., C.J. joined his fellow veterans in setting up his booth at the Link Lake Farmers' Market. The market had become of the group's significant sources of income, along with the sales at their store and the contract with the Eat Well Café. The farmers' market was similar to the cattle fairs C.J.'s grandfather had described attending when he was a young farmer, featuring not just fresh produce but also livestock and smaller animals. One veteran had a dozen forty-pound feeder pigs for sale that were meant to be fed up to two hundred pounds or so and then resold. Ben Rostom had a crate of broiler chickens, just the right size for butchering. Fresh eggs were for sale. Nearly all of the veterans, including C.J., had fresh vegetables attractively displayed. There were other goods as well: the veterans who were into woodworking presented everything from woodcarvings of old-time farmers to bluebird houses. Others offered sewing projects, wall hangings, aprons, and beautiful handmade quilts. Old Settlers Goat Cheese as well as various kinds of soaps and candles were available, all from the veteran family raising milking goats.

C.J. noticed that the sheriff was present, along with several deputies. Everyone remembered the explosion at the rhubarb festival dance.

*What will happen next?* thought C.J. *Who is so angry with us that they will do these things? And why? All we are trying to do is a little farming and, I hope, a lot of healing. Who could be opposed to that?*

By midmorning, C.J. had begun to relax a bit. If something was going to happen, it would probably have happened by now. He had even found a few minutes to talk with Maggie, who had a booth just across from his. As they were chatting, it happened.

Someone in a loud voice yelled from the far end of the market, "Look out! Coming your way."

C.J. and Maggie were immediately on high alert. What was coming their way—a threat? A killer?

Both C.J. and Maggie saw it at the same time. A pair of frightened feeder pigs had gotten out of their enclosure and were racing across the market, tipping over baskets of vegetables and generally raising havoc. When both customers and veterans realized what was happening, everyone began laughing, relieved that the "danger" was only two little pigs on the lam. Several vets surrounded the pigs, and soon their owner appeared, grabbed each squealing pig by a leg, and carried them back to the repaired enclosure.

# 24

Ames County Argus
## BACK TO THE LAND VETERANS
## RECEIVE HOMESTEAD GRANTS

Eighteen disabled veterans farming in Settlers Valley have recently signed contracts allowing them to work toward full ownership of their small-acreage farms, which range in size from five to ten acres. The Herman Barnes Family Foundation of Houston, Texas, created the Josh Barnes Memorial Homestead Fund in memory of Richard Barnes's son, who was killed in the war in Iraq. The funds are managed by the Link Lake People's Church with Pastor Victoria Emerson and C.J. Anderson, himself a disabled veteran, responsible for the administration of the grants.

In all instances, the veterans who received the grants were renting land with the provision to buy. With the grant money, veterans could now own their small-acreage farms. Oscar Anderson, longtime Settlers Valley farmer, had encouraged his farmer neighbors to rent a few acres of their farms; several of them rented more than 200 acres to disabled veterans. Floyd Steuart, the owner of 500 acres, said, "Renting five to ten acres of land to a disabled veteran is the least we could do in helping them get their feet back on the ground."

The grant was inspired by the provisions of the original Homestead Act, which was signed by President Lincoln in 1862. The 1862 law made available 160-acre plots of federally owned land to settlers who were willing to move onto the land, construct buildings and till the soil. If the settler did this successfully for five years, the land was his. Of course, the Back to the Land Veterans land acreage was much smaller than what the original Homestead Act provided.

The Josh Barnes Memorial Homestead Fund's provisions require living on the land, tilling the soil and making improvements from one year to the next. After five years, veterans who have met these minimal requirements will own their land free and clear. C.J. Anderson, who heads up the Back to the Land Veterans group, said, "This gift from the Herman Barnes Family Foundation was not expected but is so much appreciated by each and every disabled veteran."

"Well, Oscar, I guess you were right," said Fred. The two sat at their regular table at the Eat Well. "Right about this Barnes fellow from Houston," said Fred.

"Appears so," said Oscar, studying the menu to see if anything new had appeared. "You see the piece in the *Argus*?"

"I did, and I couldn't believe it. This Barnes guy must be rollin' in money," said Fred.

"I don't know about him personally, but his foundation seems to have some big bucks," said Oscar.

"No matter. It's a mighty fine thing to have these disabled vets own their own land. Nothing better than owning your own land. Gives folks an incentive to work hard," said Fred.

"Heard somethin' else too," said Oscar. "Somethin' C.J. told me the other day."

"And that would be?"

"One of the disabled vets is a better-than-average woodworker, and he made a plaque, which all the vets getting homestead land signed. On that plaque, the Back to the Land Veterans made Richard Barnes an honorary member," said Oscar.

"That was mighty good of them. Any more news, Oscar? What have you heard about the pipeline that is supposedly coming our way? Anybody heard exactly where they plan to plant that big pipe? Sure hope it's nowhere near here," said Fred.

"Nary a word," said Oscar. "I expect we should hear soon. Remember when that big electric power line company wanted to march right across our farms, right down the middle of one of my cornfields? Reminds me, too, of that goll darn sand mine that wanted to come to town."

"Do I remember? I sure do. That damn electric company thought they could stick one of them god-awful big concrete posts right next to my barn and wondered if I would mind. How dumb do these guys think we farmers are?" said Fred. "And that damn sand mine—it woulda ruined this community."

"I guess we showed 'em how dumb we weren't," chuckled Oscar. "Don't know if I'd be up to doin' all we did to keep that big transmission company off our farms if the pipeline company has a similar idea. That was twenty years ago. I'm not as young as I used to be."

"You got that right, Oscar. And neither am I. But you know, lots of people write off folks who are in their eighties as obsolete and out of touch. It'd be a mistake if this pipeline company did that. A big mistake," said Fred. Both men were chuckling as they waved the waitress over to take their orders.

# 25

As it had been his custom since he agreed to manage the Back to the Land Grocery Cooperative on Main Street, Tommy Green unlocked the front door and entered the store. At thirty-five, Tommy was the oldest of the disabled veterans who had come to Settlers Valley. He was six feet four and was built like an army tank. He had a full head of red hair and a bushy, red beard. Tommy was always friendly, with a ready smile and hearty handshake. The other businesspeople in Link Lake had quickly accepted him as one of them, inviting him to become a member of the Link Lake Business Association. Tommy and his wife, Joan, had two teenage kids, a boy and a girl. Both helped out in the store after school during the week, and one or both of them were there every Saturday.

Tommy couldn't believe what he had encountered when he opened the grocery door on this sunny day in June. Everything had been going so well. The store was selling enough to make a modest profit and offer Tommy and his family enough income for a decent living. He was pleased that he was able to help out his fellow disabled veterans living in the area. But now this. "Why?" said Tommy aloud as he punched in the number for the sheriff's office on his cell phone.

The Back to the Land Grocery Cooperative opened a year after the first disabled veterans came to Settlers Valley. By the start of year three, every one of the twenty in the valley grew vegetables for sale, although several had other enterprises as well, such as beekeeping, free-range hogs, milking goats, chickens, and growing hops and hemp. A couple of the vets, in their home kitchens, baked bread, sweet rolls, and pies for sale in the store. At least three of the vets were, in addition to their small-acreage farming, making a variety of wood products, including woodcarvings. Several of the women were into decorative quilt making and other sewing projects. An area in the back of the store was devoted to these materials. A small office in the far end of the store, with an outside entrance, housed the offices for the Back to the Land Veterans. So the BTTL Grocery Cooperative was much more than a grocery store. But now something dreadful had happened. Tommy Green sat on a little stool behind the cash register, not touching anything, waiting for the sheriff to arrive.

At one of the group's first meetings two years ago, they had discussed the market potential for not just fresh vegetables but also free-range hogs, chickens, honey, goat milk cheese, and canning and baking products. They had fared well selling these products at the Link Lake Farmers' Market from April through October. But they would need a year-round source of income, and they would need goods to sell in the winter months.

The group agreed that a year-round grocery would be a good idea, but how would they finance it and who would run the store? It was C.J. who remembered Tommy Green, whom he had met at Walter Reed. He recalled suggesting Tommy come to Settlers Valley and take up farming. "I know nothing about farming," Tommy had said. "I grew up working in my dad's grocery store in Williston, North Dakota." As the group's plans for a grocery store had taken shape, C.J. had gotten in touch with Tommy, and, with a little arm-twisting, convinced him to be its manager. Tommy had said, "I'm not so sure my kids are impressed that they would be following in their father's footsteps, but they seem to think working in a grocery store might be fun."

The group set up the store as a cooperative, with each member owning a share and additional shares selling for a hundred dollars each. Oscar Anderson was the one who recommended they contact Clyde Goring, a Vietnam vet who had been trying for some time to sell his grocery store in Link Lake. Clyde had agreed to rent the store and all of its equipment to the cooperative, with the option to purchase the store when they were financially stable.

Oscar, who had spent his entire life in the Link Lake community, knew about Clyde's Grocery, which had quit operations a few months earlier. Clyde had been trying to sell the grocery but had no takers. It was often said, "If Clyde couldn't make a living in the store, nobody could."

When C.J. talked to Clyde about creating a new kind of grocery cooperative and told him they didn't have enough money to buy the store, Clyde, being a Vietnam vet, agreed to rent the store and all its equipment to the cooperative.

With Oscar's help, C.J. had prepared an announcement to send to the local newspaper.

*Ames County Argus*
SETTLERS VALLEY DISABLED VETS OPEN
GROCERY COOPERATIVE

The Back to the Land Veterans, made up of disabled military veterans who are establishing small-acreage farms in Settlers Valley near Link Lake, are opening a grocery cooperative in the former Clyde's Grocery building on Main Street in Link Lake.

Spokesman C.J. Anderson said, "The Back to the Land Veterans are thrilled to be able to open a grocery store in Link Lake. The veterans plan to offer fresh vegetables and fruits, most of which will be grown on the veterans' small-acreage farms. The store will also sell fresh bakery goods baked at two of the vets' farms as well as home-canned fruits and vegetables. Various craft projects created by the veterans, including woodcarvings and handmade quilts, will be available for sale as well.

Clyde Goring, who operated Clyde's Grocery on the site for more than two decades, has agreed to help the new store get started.

Anyone interested in purchasing a share in this new local food cooperative should contact C.J. Anderson. The Back to the Land Veterans are pleased to provide this unique service to the community, assuring customers of a steady supply of locally grown and preserved fruits and vegetables as well as free-range poultry and pork products, plus various veteran-created craft goods.

Fifteen minutes after Tommy's call, Sheriff Jansen arrived at the store. "What's going on, Tommy?" he asked.

"See for yourself, Sheriff," said Tommy.

"Jeez," said the sheriff as he glanced around to see vegetables spilled all over the floor—freshly picked peas, early beets, radishes, onions, lettuce—in a tangled mess. What looked like several gallons of milk had been dumped on top of the vegetables. A beautiful handmade quilt, with a red barn and farmhouse sewn into the design, had been virtually destroyed and tossed on the pile of vegetables.

"Who would do such a thing?" asked Tommy. "These are vegetables grown by disabled vets trying to make a living on their small-acreage farms. I know the vet who sewed this quilt. It took her hours to make it, and she was so proud. She was reluctant to display it here at the store. What in the world do I tell her?"

"I think I discovered how someone got into the store," said Sheriff Jansen. He had been checking doors and windows. "Somebody jimmied the lock on your delivery door." He and Tommy inspected the broken lock.

"Any way to find out who did this?" Tommy asked.

"We'll open an investigation," said Sheriff Jansen. "In the meantime, I would recommend a couple of things. First, buy some better locks, and second, you'll want to invest in some security cameras. If this happens again, and I sure hope it doesn't, at least you'll be able to see who did it. Is any money missing?"

"Far as I can tell not a dime is missing. Weird, isn't it? Whoever did this wasn't after money. In fact, it doesn't look like the culprit stole anything at all."

# 26

Lucy James sat alone in her office at the Link Lake School on a warm mid-June day. Despite her worries, the eighth-grade and senior graduation ceremonies had gone off without a hitch. Lucy had seen many changes in her twenty years heading up the Link Lake school system. One of the first changes she had advocated for and had approved by the school board was year-round schooling. The school operated for four quarters of forty-five days each, and each quarter was followed by fifteen days of vacation. There had been some pushback from parents who believed that their students should have the entire summer off. But that controversy was nothing compared to the past few years when the Link Lake community split itself into warring factions—those who supported the relatively new Link Lake People's Church and those opposed to it; those who supported the Back to the Land Veterans and those who opposed them. The students, even down to the little ones in kindergarten, seemed to be choosing sides, just as their parents were doing, reflecting the attitudes and actions of their parents. Before these last couple of years, student fights were a rarity. Now, it seemed almost every day some kid was in dispute with another one, over some disagreement.

*So much hatred. So much choosing sides,* Lucy thought as she finished working on end-of-the-year reports. Lucy had grown up on a farm in the Link Lake community. She remembered how, when she was growing up, all the farmers in the area, no matter their religion or political beliefs, worked together, played together, and indeed enjoyed each other's company. Even when they had disagreements, they agreed more with each other than they disagreed.

Lucy James was proud of what their little school, with a total student population of five hundred students in K–12, all in the same building, had accomplished over the twenty years she had been principal. But now she worried about the fights, the arguments, the anger many students were expressing. The school forest and its big vegetable garden were bright spots. The school garden and school forest were where students learned to work together no matter if they had disagreements and differences in beliefs. Not only was the school forest a living laboratory that all students visited at least twice a year, in the fall and again in the spring, and often in summer, too, but Link Lake students had also restored about five acres of prairie on the 200-acre site.

Lucy was most proud of the school's quarter-acre vegetable garden adjacent to the restored prairie and near the shelter house. She read about school gardens providing learning opportunities for students who worked the soil, and how the resulting vegetables grown could enhance the school lunch program. She read about tiny little gardens, sometimes in raised beds only four by six feet, and was impressed with how many vegetables such as green beans and lettuce could be grown in so little space. Lucy remembered helping her parents with her family's vegetable garden, and she wanted the school's garden to be like the one she grew up with. The school forestland provided the space to do it.

Lucy recalled when she took her idea to a school board meeting five years ago. She introduced the topic by sharing what other schools had recently done with school gardens. She stressed that students would be doing much of the work, providing opportunities for them to learn some essential skills, such as how to take care of the land, how to grow vegetables, and how to work together with a common goal.

"Sounds interesting," school board president Glen Mosston had said. "But what's it going to cost? You know we're always short of money for the important things: math, reading, science—these are the areas where we should be putting any spare money we can scrape up."

"I don't want to do what many of the urban schools have been doing, developing a small garden plot near the school," Lucy explained. "I want to have a school garden in an open area we have at the school forest. Regarding cost, I know some retired farmers in the area who will help us get started at no cost. And the vegetables we grow there can replace vegetables we are now buying for our school lunch program so we'll save some money there."

"I don't know about this," Mosston had said. "Sounds a little like another educational fad."

"If I could offer a comment," broke in Sandie Dixman. "I support Lucy's idea. I have a garden at home, and although my kids don't always like working in it, I know they are learning a lot from doing it. All the way from something as simple as pulling weeds to learning how to test soil—and learning how to work."

"I don't know, Sandie. Don't the students here in Link Lake have vegetable gardens at home, like you do?" asked Mosston.

"I did a little checking," Lucy said. "I asked our elementary teachers to ask their students how many had vegetable gardens at home. Frankly, I was surprised. It amounted to only about ten percent of them. That's all."

After a half hour of additional discussion, the seven-member board voted. Four favored Lucy's garden idea and three were opposed. With the go-ahead, Lucy moved forward. She first talked with Joe Berry, one of the school's janitors, about her idea. Joe was a retired farmer, and Lucy knew that he still raised a big vegetable garden.

"Joe," she had said, upon seeing him working in the hall the morning following the vote, "could you step into my office for a minute?" Joe Berry was tall and thin, with a full head of white hair and gray eyes that could drill right through you—or at least that's what students who had been caught by Mr. Berry making some mischief said about him.

"Sure," said Joe, wondering if he had done something wrong.

"You used to farm," Lucy began.

"Yup, for more than thirty years. The wife and I sold the place and moved to town."

"Did you grow vegetables?" Lucy asked.

Joe began to wonder where this conversation was headed.

"Of course, we always had a big vegetable garden. Had fresh vegetables all summer long. Frozen vegetables in the winter."

Lucy told Joe about the school board's decision to allow her to plow up a quarter acre or so of open land in the school forest and plant a vegetable garden. "Would you be able to help me with this project?" she asked.

"Sure," answered Joe without hesitation. "I'd be happy to help."

From that day forward, Joe Berry, in addition to his janitorial duties at the school, had been the unofficial director of the Link Lake school garden.

# 27

A knock came on the principal's office door. "Come in," said Lucy. The door opened and Joe Berry entered.

"Am I early?" Joe asked.

"No, no," said Lucy. "I'm ready. And I'm really looking forward to spending a couple days out of the office."

Joe and Lucy got into Joe's pickup, and they headed to the school forest and vegetable garden for the annual eighth-grade post-graduation party and workday.

"So how's the garden doing, Joe?" asked Lucy as they drove along.

"Remarkably well," said Joe. "Rains came at the right time this year. Looks like we'll have the best potato crop ever. The tomatoes are looking good. Green beans have been great. And lettuce, I can't remember when our green lettuce crop looked better. Kale, well this is the first year we've grown it, and we can't cut it fast enough."

"Glad to hear it. Kids doing okay with the weed pulling and hoeing?"

"Lots of bickering. Don't remember kids arguing with each other so much. Kids probably sayin' what they're hearin' from their folks," said Joe.

"Yup, that's what happening these days. I can't remember so many fights in school. Even caught a kid with a .22 rifle in his locker. It wasn't loaded. Kid said he brought it to school to scare off a kid who was picking on him. Been a tough year. I was hoping that a little garden work might bring the kids together," said Lucy.

"It helps," said Joe.

The eighth-graders were scheduled to arrive at the school garden site shortly after noon. They would work in the garden for a couple of hours, then hike the trails in the prairie and woods, enjoy a picnic at day's end, and finally—before going to sleep in the tents provided by the Boy Scouts—gather around a campfire and share the adventures of the day.

Before the school bus arrived with the eighth-graders, Joe and Lucy walked out to the garden. Joe wanted Lucy to see firsthand what the students had accomplished so far this year. Students worked periodically in the garden all summer since the school operated year-round.

"It really does look good this year," said Lucy. She inspected the several rows of potatoes that were thriving. "Say, Joe. Looks like something has been digging up a few hills of potatoes."

"That's happened before. Likely a woodchuck or maybe a raccoon crawled under the electric fence and helped themselves. I noticed another time that a foot or so of leaf lettuce seemed to have been eaten. I suppose we could add another wire to the electric fence, closer to the ground—but it's a little late in the season, and it's a lot of work to do. Besides, I'm not sure that our solar-powered electric charger could handle a third wire."

Just then the big yellow-and-black school bus pulled into the school forest parking lot and thirty eighth-graders piled out. Joe welcomed them and turned off the electric fence as the young people found their favorite garden hoes. Joe assigned them in pairs of two to the garden rows that needed hoeing, while he manned the rototiller that he worked between the rows. Lucy, not unfamiliar with a garden hoe, joined the students in the garden. They worked quietly, talking among themselves and not demonstrating any of the bickering and name-calling that she had heard so much during the year.

By three o'clock, they had finished the garden work. Lucy led the group on a tour of the prairie, one of her personal favorite places. She stopped by a clump of tall grass, with leaves that had a bluish tinge.

"Anybody know the name for this tall grass?" Lucy asked.

"It's big bluestem," one of the girls said, proudly. "I remember Mr. Berry showing us that grass when I was here one other time."

"You are correct," said Lucy, smiling. "Settlers that came to this place in the mid-1800s saw lots of big bluestem. The roots go as deep below ground as the grass grows above it."

"See those birdhouses?" said Lucy, pointing to a row of a dozen birdhouses that stood atop wooden posts along one side of the prairie. "Your fellow students in our school shop built them. What kind of birds nest in these houses?"

"Robins," a student said quietly.

"Sparrows?" another student offered.

"These houses were built for bluebirds," Lucy said. "At the time we put up those houses, almost no bluebirds lived here. About half of the birdhouses now have bluebirds in them. What other birds use the nesting boxes?" Lucy asked.

Silence.

"Tree swallows," Lucy said, answering her own question. "An equally beautiful bird."

The group hiked on until it came to a far corner of the restored prairie, to a little south- facing side hill. There they came upon a cluster of wildflowers that nearly covered the ground, a patch maybe fifty by fifty yards in size.

"Anybody know what these flowers are?" asked Lucy, bending over and cupping one of the purple flowers in her hand.

"Are they . . . are they lupines?" a quiet little eighth-grade girl asked.

"Yes, you are correct. These are wild lupines. They're related to the garden peas that grow in our school garden. I first noticed this patch of lupines three or four years ago, and each year the patch has gotten bigger," said Lucy.

By five o'clock everyone gathered around the picnic tables, where caterers had laid out a picnic supper of grilled hamburgers and bratwurst, potato salad, and chocolate cake. Although tired from all the activity, the students seemed to be having a good time as they celebrated their eighth-grade graduation and looked forward to high school.

Meanwhile, Joe Berry had started a campfire in the council ring that was surrounded by logs cut from the school forest. A few parents arrived to stay with the children overnight.

Lucy led a discussion with several questions, beginning with, "Is anyone tired?" All hands went up. She then asked each student to say one thing that described their afternoon in the garden and hiking trails. She heard: "Awesome," "Hard work," "Fun day," "Good to be outdoors," "Beautiful place," and similar comments.

It had just begun to get dark. The campfire was burning down when the group heard a sound: "Whip-poor-will, Whip-poor-will" called again and again from the direction of the prairie. When Lucy asked the students what bird it was, most were able to answer, as the whip-poor-will calls its own name on warm nights in spring and summer. Lucy told the children that the bird's numbers were in decline and that they were privileged to be able to hear it.

As the last bit of daylight disappeared and the only light was that of the dying campfire, the group sat quietly, listening to the sounds of the evening. Several of them jumped when they heard a roar coming from deep in the woods.

"What was that?" a frightened boy asked.

"Just some wild creature," said Lucy, not wanting to alarm the children. But she couldn't identify the sound.

Then came a roar, this time even louder and closer. The students, most of them frightened out of their wits, raced to the safety of the shelter house. Lucy followed behind, wondering what kind of animal had invaded the school forest. It would be a while before her question would be answered.

# 28

*Ames County Argus*
PIPELINE DECISION IMMINENT

The *Argus* has learned that the Al-Mid Pipeline Company will make a final decision about where the pipeline will be sited by late July. Emory Sage, field representative for the company, said, "We have selected two possible sites in Ames County for the new Al-Mid Pipeline, which will bring thousands of barrels of crude oil from Canada to the refineries near Chicago."

When asked if he could be more specific, Sage said, "We are considering one possible route that will take the pipeline just east of Link Lake. A second possible route runs the pipeline through Settlers Valley. Each potential route has its advantages and disadvantages."

The *Argus* contacted John Wilson, who operates a large farm in the region and is currently president of the local Eagle Party, for his thoughts about the pipeline, especially if it might wish to cross his property.

"First," Wilson said, "I am absolutely thrilled that the pipeline will be crossing Ames County and located near Link Lake. Pipelines are the safest, easiest and most cost-efficient way of moving petroleum products from one place to another. This will be one more way of our country easily getting oil."

Wilson went on to say that he would have no problem if the pipeline chose a route across his farm. "I would applaud it," he said.

"Well, Oscar, how are you on this beautiful June day? Just can't beat the month of June. A great month," said Fred as he reached for his coffee cup. Oscar had just arrived and pulled up a chair across from Fred at their Eat Well Café reserved table.

"I'm fine, and June is not my favorite month, it's October," said Oscar.

"Well, aren't you the grump on this glorious day," said a smiling Fred.

"You read the latest issue of the *Argus*?"

"I have not," said Fred. "Just too darn busy. Lots goin' on in June. Too busy to keep up with my readin'."

"Well, you better read it, Fred. You'd better read it," said Oscar.

"Some juicy gossip, somebody get caught runnin' off with somebody else's wife?"

"Jeez, Fred, when was the last time you read in the paper about somebody runnin' off with someone else's wife?"

"Not too long ago I read that. Don't recall the guy's name, but he got caught speedin'—and if I remember correctly, he had the Willow Creek mayor's wife in the car with him. Bad luck for him. Not too good news for the mayor either."

"Well, what I read . . ." Oscar hesitated as a massive stack of pancakes appeared before both him and Fred.

"What I read," Oscar continued, "is that Settlers Valley may be selected for the proposed pipeline."

"To hell, you say," said Fred before taking a big bite from the pancake stack in front of him.

"You gotta read it yourself, Fred. It's all right there in black and white," said Oscar.

"So what are we gonna do about it?"

"Nothin' until I hear for sure. The article said the pipeline company's gonna decide by the end of the month," said Oscar.

"What can we do right now?" asked Fred.

"One thing you can do is start readin' the paper," said Oscar, smiling.

"With all the problems this community has these days, we sure don't need no damn pipeline coming through here. That's the last thing we need," said Fred.

"You're sure right about that," said Oscar as he took another sip of coffee. "These disabled vets are all workin' hard and doin' pretty well. And I must say learnin' how to farm faster than I thought they would. They surely don't need any more challenges. Let's see. First, there was the burnin' of their church, then the fracas at my barn, and who can forget what happened the first night of the rhubarb festival when the lights went out and somebody set off one of them aerial bombs. And just a short time ago, somebody came in and trashed the little grocery store the vets opened up on Main Street in Link Lake. Just one thing after the other." He shook his head.

"Sheriff had any luck findin' out who's been doin' all this stuff?" asked Fred.

"Haven't heard. C.J. would know. I talk to him almost every day, and he hasn't mentioned it. C.J. did tell me that Maggie Werch is workin' part-time as a consultant for the sheriff."

"She the one that C.J. has taken a shine to?"

"Yup, she's the one," said Oscar. "She's really pretty nice."

"Well, good for C.J.," said Fred. "Every man needs a woman in his life."

The two men sat quietly for a time, enjoying their second cups of coffee.

"I learned somethin' weird the other day," began Fred.

"Weird, huh. You look in the mirror?" said Oscar, chuckling.

"Oscar, can you be serious for a minute?"

"I am serious. I'm a serious guy. You don't believe it, just ask me."

"You know Joe Berry; he used to farm east of Link Lake. He's retired and now works as a janitor at the Link Lake School," said Fred.

"Yeah, I know Joe. He trip over his broom?"

"No, he didn't. You probably didn't know that he is also in charge of the garden that the school grows out at the school forest property."

"I didn't know that," said Oscar, waiting for Fred to get to the point.

"I was talkin' to Joe at the gas station the other day, and he told me about what he saw when he was out to the school garden the other day."

"And that would be . . . ?" asked Oscar.

"Joe saw several hills of potatoes had been dug up, some leaf lettuce had been cut, and some radishes pulled."

"So, a groundhog got into the garden and helped itself to an easy meal."

"That's what Joe believed at first, and then the more he thought about it, he now believes somebody is stealin' vegetables from the school garden."

"Really?" offered Oscar. "That is weird. Who in the world would steal vegetables from a garden?"

"Joe's gonna find out. He's settin' up one of those trail cameras. He strapped it to a tree, placed it so you've gotta look to see it, he told me. Who or what is stealin' from the garden will have its picture took," said Fred.

# 29

The Village of Link Lake enjoyed its celebrations. The Fourth of July celebration was the premier event, drawing more people than the rhubarb festival, Memorial Day, and Labor Day combined. Remembering Link Lake's roots had become a town tradition on the Fourth of July. Various people recited bits and pieces of the history of Link Lake, which was founded by Increase Joseph Link of New York State in 1852. This year C.J. asked U.S. senator Sam Shelburne from Maine to speak at the festivities. Senator Shelburne, a Vietnam vet and disabled veterans advocate, had become aware of the Back to the Land Veterans farming in Settlers Valley and had mentioned the group in his weekly blogs. When asked if he might come to Link Lake, his response was quick and decisive: "I would love to come to Link Lake and speak and see firsthand what this disabled veterans group is doing."

The Fourth of July parade was always a highlight of the celebration. But it would not happen this year. Sheriff Jansen had written the following to the planning committee: "In light of recent tragic events in the greater Link Lake community, including the burning of a church and other disruptive activities, and with the culprit or culprits still on the loose, I must say no to your Fourth of July parade. The Sheriff's Department simply does not have enough resources to assure that it will be a safe event."

The Fourth of July dawned clear, sunny, and hot, with the temperature expected to crawl into the low nineties by midafternoon, when the various speakers were to give their presentations. Just about every local organization had a booth or a display of some kind, lined up on both sides of Link Lake's Main Street, which had been closed to vehicular traffic. First in line was the booth sponsored by the Church of the Holy Redeemed. Pastor Jacob John Jacob, dressed all in black with coat and tie, along with three women from his church, greeted people who walked by, announcing a blessing to those who stopped for a moment to examine their materials displayed on a table in front of them. Next to them sat the Link Lake Woodcarvers, a half-dozen older gentlemen showing off some of their carving projects and giving demonstrations. The Link Lake Hookers, a group of women who hooked rugs, was next. Of course, the Link Lake Pub and Brew had a brisk business on this warmer-than-average July afternoon. The Eat Well staff was grilling bratwurst and hamburgers, sending the wonderful smell of grilling meat down Main Street. The Ames County Eagle Party had an enormous booth, with American flags everywhere. John Wilson, Eagle Party president, sat behind a bowl of little flags that he passed out to all who walked by. Now and again someone would stop to talk with Wilson, who readily shared his concerns about what was happening in the Link Lake community and his hope that Eagle Party representatives would soon be elected to "cure the many ills that Link Lake was experiencing these days."

The Back to the Land Veterans had a large booth, where several of the veterans, their spouses, and their children took turns talking to folks who stopped by and wanted to learn more about them and their work on small-acreage farms. The Link Lake People's Church booth was adjacent to the vets' booth.

Sheriff Jansen was there, concerned as usual that something drastic might happen on this hot day with several hundred people walking along Main Street in Link Lake. Five of his deputies were with him, posted at what the sheriff considered strategic places to prevent any disruption of the celebration. Maggie Werch was also on duty. By noon, the sheriff relaxed a bit. He assumed that temperatures in the nineties might help to prevent any skullduggery from occurring.

A speaker's stand was erected on the sidewalk in front of the Eat Well Café, with a podium and an American flag with a brass eagle perched on top of the  flagpole standing next to it. The first speaker of the day was Emily Higgins, president of the Link Lake Historical Society.

Emily, a short, thin, gray-haired women in her eighties, ambled up to the stand and with a loud, clear voice began, "Welcome to Link Lake's annual Fourth of July celebration. It's a bit on the warm side today, but for many of us, the Fourth of July means a warm day. I'm here to say a few words about our village's history, which goes back to 1852, when preacher Increase Joseph and his little band of followers arrived here from New York State, where they had been living and worshipping." She paused for a moment and took a drink of water. "Increase Joseph, as we commonly refer to him, was a remarkable man. He was not only a man of the cloth, but he was a man of the land. He believed that we, as residents of the community, may have different origins, different beliefs, and different ways of doing things, but we must learn to get along with one another and appreciate one another. I want to share with you a few of his words to give you the flavor of his thinking:

> We are each of us like the giant oaks . . . The oak lives in harmony with its neighbors, the aspen, the maple, and the pines, as we each must also learn to live with those who are different from us.
> We must learn to live in harmony with the Norwegians and the Welsh, the Swedes and the Danes, the Irish and the English, the Poles and the Germans, and the Indians. . . . All are our neighbors.

We must learn to live with those whose work is different from ours. We must learn to live with those who worship in ways foreign to us. There is one God, and he is concerned about all of us, no matter how we choose to honor Him. He wants us to prosper, wants us to get along with each other, but first, he wants us to respect the land. We must always remember that the land comes first. We must learn how to take care of the land or we all shall perish.

Loud applause followed.

C.J. Anderson was next to speak.

"I represent the Back to the Land Veterans. We are small-acreage farmers living and working in Settlers Valley. Each of us fought for this country and fought for this flag." C.J. turned toward the flag. "We fought for independence of our country that the Fourth of July celebrates." His words were punctuated with loud and sustained applause.

"Along with Miss Higgins, I too want to quote a few lines from Increase Joseph's work, which the Link Lake Historical Society under her direction has so well preserved. These are Increase Joseph's words:

I dreamed of a time when people cared for the land as the land cared for them. A time when people took care of each other as God takes care of each of us. A time when all of God's creatures, the birds and the animals, the trees and the wildflowers, the air we breathe and the water we drink, the very soil we walk on became one with us.

We are all part of the land, have been and forever will be. As farmers, it is our God-given task to care for the land, to till it, nourish it, protect it, and above all give it respect. In return, the land will feed us, embrace us, and give us the joy that comes with a bountiful harvest.

"This is what our group of disabled veterans is trying to do. These words guide us, give us courage, and give us hope. Thank you very much."

The applause was loud and long.

C.J. continued. "Now it is my privilege to introduce our special guest. He comes to us from the great state of Maine. He, like me and many of you, is a military veteran—he fought in Vietnam. It is my great pleasure to introduce to you United States senator Sam Shelburne."

Senator Shelburne, tall, thin, with a full head of gray hair, got up from his chair and walked to the podium. He retrieved a pair of glasses from his shirt pocket, adjusted them, and then looked out over the audience, which stood silently, wondering what he had to say but hoping his talk would be short as the day had gotten progressively warmer.

"It is my great pleasure to be here today and to be a part of your Fourth of July celebration," the senator began. "This day is important for us. It is a day away from work for most of you, and a chance to eat potato salad and feast on Wisconsin's famous bratwurst." He smiled when he said it and pointed toward the Eat Well's brat stand, where heavy smoke from the grill nearly hid the people working there.

"But we must not forget what we are celebrating," the senator said as he swiped his forehead with a handkerchief. "On this day we celebrate our country's independence." He pointed to the American flag with the big brass eagle fixed to the top of the flag stand that stood a few inches from where he was speaking. "This is the day that our forefathers decided enough was enough. I want to read the Preamble to the Declaration of Independence—something you've probably not heard since you were in grade school."

The senator removed a piece of paper from his pocket and unfolded it. He began reading.

We hold these truths to be self-evident, that all men are created equal, that they are endowed by their Creator with certain unalienable Rights, that among these are Life, Liberty and the pursuit of Happiness. That to secure these rights, Governments are instituted among Men, deriving their just powers from the consent of the governed.

"It was on July 4, 1776, that the Continental Congress approved these words and signed the document on August 2 of that year," said the senator in his deep baritone voice. "These words, so powerfully penned by Thomas Jefferson, set this great nation on its way. These words—" He did not finish his sentence. The brass eagle on top of the flag stand exploded in a thousand pieces, a few of them striking the senator. Then came a loud "pop," which C.J. immediately identified as a rifle shot. C.J. dove for the senator, pinning him to the temporary plywood floor of the speaker's stand and covering him for fear a second shot would find its mark.

For a moment there was silence, complete silence. And then a woman standing immediately in front of the raised podium screamed, shattering the quiet, followed by another scream. People began running, stumbling against each other, falling down, crawling, and doing everything they could to move from their places in front of the speakers stand. Then sirens, several sirens. Chaos. Profound and complete confusion.

"Are you hurt?" asked C.J. as he helped the senator from the podium to a seat under a tree a few yards away.

"I . . . I don't think so. Just a couple little cuts on my arm. Was it a gunshot?" he asked with a shaky voice.

"I believe so," said C.J., who had begun wiping blood from the senator's arm.

"Was it meant for me?"

"Probably," answered C.J. "The shooter missed. But not by much."

# 30

Maggie Werch and Sheriff Jansen were standing together off to one side of the crowd when they saw the eagle on top of the flag stand explode and they heard the pop, which they both immediately identified as gunfire. *Sniper*, Maggie instantly thought. The sheriff sprinted toward the podium and then saw C.J. tending to the senator, who was sitting under a tree. Maggie ran in the direction of the shot, having heard similar shots when she was on active duty in the army.

She raced down the already mostly cleared Main Street, searching for places where a sniper might have been. She knew that trained snipers could hit a target as small as a metal eagle perched on top of a flag stand or, heaven forbid, the senator's head from several hundred yards away. She wondered why or how the sniper had missed its target.

She sprinted what she assumed to be about three hundred yards, still a comfortable range for a trained sniper, looking at the roofs of buildings along the way, hoping to spot someone, hoping to locate the sniper, who would surely be on the run. Then she saw an open window on the second floor of what had once been the Link Lake Hotel but was now mostly used as storage space. Arriving at the building, she tried the door. Unlocked, she pushed inside, on alert. She carried her loaded 9mm Beretta in her purse. Now she took it out.

She spotted a stairway in the back of what had been the old hotel's lobby, which was now a clutter of bird and animal droppings, pieces of old newspaper, and cobwebs, lots of cobwebs, which she brushed from her face. She stopped to listen and heard nothing except the twittering of an English sparrow. She started up the stairway, her Beretta at the ready. At the top of the first flight of stairs, she stopped and listened. Then she heard footsteps on the floor above her. She continued quickly but silently up the second flight of stairs, thankful that she was in as good shape as she had been when she was in the service. *Thank God, working on a farm has kept me fit,* she thought. But she quickly refocused. She learned that in the military: keep focused on your mission, or you may be the next casualty.

Reaching the second-floor hallway, she saw a man dressed all in black running down the hall toward the emergency stairs in the back of the old hotel.

"Stop or I'll shoot!" she yelled at the running figure. But the man didn't stop and Maggie didn't shoot as he disappeared in the stairwell on the other end of the hall. Maggie yelled at him, "Stop! I've got a gun!" She hurried down the back stairs, hoping to catch up with the man she assumed was the shooter. Then she saw him disappear into the crowd of frightened spectators. She returned to the room where the window was open and discovered where the sniper had been positioned. She had found the location of the shooter quickly, so quickly that he didn't have time to disassemble his sniper rifle, which lay on the floor, a spent bullet casing next to it. Maggie quickly recognized the rifle. It was a Winchester .300 caliber with a scope, almost identical to the military version known as an M-24 rifle. She left the weapon where it lay. She looked out the open window that faced Main Street; she could clearly see the podium in the distance. "Easy shot," she said aloud. *Why had he missed?* Maggie thought again.

On the floor, next to the rifle, she spotted a black book. She looked more closely and saw the words *Holy Bible.* Next to the Bible was a small, hand-lettered placard, "Sinners Deserve to Die," scrawled in what looked like red paint. The would-be killer had obviously left these items for someone to find.

Maggie tucked her Beretta back in her purse and hurried back to where the sheriff and C.J. were talking with the senator, who was sipping on a bottle of water.

"Have you had any death threats or threats of any kind?" Maggie overheard the sheriff ask.

"No, not recently. But, but lots of people don't like what I stand for. Some of these people can be violent. First time I've been shot at though," the senator said, his voice still shaking.

Maggie said to the sheriff, "Can I have a word with you?"

The two moved off to the side as Maggie explained that she had confronted the shooter and had found the place where he fired the shot.

"C.J, would you stay with the senator while I go with Maggie?" Sheriff Jensen asked.

"Sure," C.J. said as he watched Maggie and the sheriff hurry away. C.J. had been impressed to see Maggie in action. *This is a side of Maggie Werch I have not seen before. Professional, in charge, no-nonsense,* C.J. thought. He had come to know Maggie as a young woman eager to learn about farming, a young woman who was tender, caring, and loving—and who seemed to enjoy being with him, as he now spent more nights in her bed than he did at his own cabin.

"Anything I can do for you, Senator?" C.J. asked.

"Yes, get me the hell out of here before somebody else attacks me." Now C.J. was seeing a side of the senator he had not seen.

After reviewing the sniper's nest, as Maggie described it, the sheriff put on gloves and carefully picked up the sniper rifle and the spent shell case. "This may be the break we've wanted," he said. "Let's hope there're some fingerprints on this weapon and we can trace it back to where the shooter bought it. My guess is that this is the same guy who caused all the other trouble the past few months. Good work, Maggie."

"Thank you," Maggie said, smiling. "Just trying to earn my consulting fee."

# 31

By day's end, the press had swooped down on Link Lake, Wisconsin, like a hawk swoops down on an unlucky field mouse. TV stations from Wausau, Green Bay, and Madison arrived first. They parked their trucks along Main Street. By midevening a reporter for the *New York Chronicle* had come, the *Washington News* was not far behind, and of course a news team from CNO set up a portable studio a yard or two from where the shooting had taken place. All were looking for a sensational story on what had been a quiet Fourth of July across the country. An attempted assassination of a well-known U.S. senator was news—the kind of story that would draw people to their cell phones and TV screens, that would sell newspapers, like the good old days when something sensational boosted paper sales.

Headlines on the July 5 edition of the *Washington News* shouted: "Popular U.S. Senator Survives Assassination Attempt." The *New York Chronicle* spread this headline across the top of its front page: "U.S. Senator Sam Shelburne Injured in Fourth of July Shooting."

CNO had reporters busily interviewing whomever they could find. They soon convened a panel of "experts" discussing "violence in small-town America." An editorial writer in the Eagle Party's *National Eagle News* wrote:

Violence and assassination have moved from the major cities into the small towns of America. Little bucolic Link Lake, located in sparsely populated Ames County, Wisconsin, was visited during its Fourth of July celebration by a vicious killer who nearly succeeded in assassinating a U.S. senator.

The would-be killer, more than likely an undocumented alien, has not been captured. America will not be safe until all of these would-be killers are either jailed or deported. When will the nation wake up to the fact that it has a problem of enormous proportions? The country cannot continue on its present course when law-abiding, hardworking citizens do not feel safe attending time-honored celebrations such as the Fourth of July.

The local newspaper carried a front-page editorial with a photo of Senator Shelburne sitting under a tree with C.J. kneeling in front of him.

*Ames County Argus*
ASSASSINATION ATTEMPT OF ADVOCATE
FOR DISABLED VETERANS
Bill Baxter, Managing Editor

U.S. senator Sam Shelburne, Maine, a longtime advocate for disabled veterans and himself a Vietnam Veteran, narrowly missed an assassin's bullet as he spoke at the Fourth of July celebration in Link Lake. As many of our readers know, Settlers Valley, located west of Link Lake, is the site of an experiment designed to help disabled military veterans who have been profoundly injured both mentally and physically. Calling themselves the Back to the Land Veterans, some 20 of them and their families have taken up small-acreage farming in Settlers Valley. They are following the long-known adage, long known but seldom spoken these days, "As we heal the land, the land will heal us." These veterans are practicing land use approaches that have more often been set aside by the industrial-size farms that have been springing up throughout the country, including Ames County. These young farmers, most of them in their twenties and thirties, are being assisted by retired farmers Fred Russo and Oscar Anderson and Anderson's grandson, C.J. Anderson, a disabled veteran himself.

There is considerable anecdotal evidence that the experiment is working and that these young farmers injured by the war are healing. The land they farm, in prior years devoted to corn crop after corn crop until the fields appeared as dead as a windswept desert, seems to be healing as well.

Not only are these young farmers producing food for themselves, but they are making their homegrown food available to whomever stops by their grocery cooperative, located on Main Street in Link Lake, or attend the regular Saturday farmers' market in Link Lake.

Learning about the Back to the Land Veterans, a former military chaplain, Victoria Emerson, who has experience counseling veterans suffering from post-traumatic stress disorder (PTSD), moved to Link Lake and organized the Link Lake People's Church, which many of the veterans attend. Unfortunately, the Back to the Land Veterans experiment, which appeared to be a winning idea for all concerned, is not seen that way by a swath of Ames County citizens. Some have called the church anti-Christian. It was burned to the ground and is currently being rebuilt with funds donated by the public. Some have called the disabled veterans' approach to farming as a step backward and a challenge to the progress agriculture has made during the past three decades. These advances in agriculture have resulted in increased crop production per acre; increased milk production per cow; fewer days necessary to produce hogs, poultry and beef for market; and all with the smallest number of people working in agriculture in the history of the country.

The Back to the Land Veterans group is nonviolent. Its members believe, as did Martin Luther King Jr., that violence begets violence. No member of the disabled vets' group speaks negatively about anyone. Love thy neighbor as thyself is a motto not so much spoken as practiced.

This brings us to the unanswered question. Who is so angry with the Back to the Land Veterans that they would attempt to assassinate a national advocate for disabled veterans?

The following Friday evening, C.J. took Maggie out for her birthday. They decided to drive to Oshkosh as an attempt to get away from all the lingering publicity that continued to swirl around Link Lake concerning the now infamous Fourth of July celebration. C.J. drove them the forty-five minutes to the Lake View Supper Club, located on the shores of beautiful Lake Winnebago, Wisconsin's largest inland lake. They talked little as they drove, each with their own thoughts of what happened a few days ago.

When they arrived at the supper club, they were immediately seated at a table overlooking the lake.

"What will you have to drink?" asked the waitress who soon appeared at their table.

"Water will be fine," said C.J.

"Water for me too," said Maggie.

"Well," began C.J. "It was quite a week."

"You're right about that," said Maggie. "What do you make of all the news coverage? If little Link Lake wasn't on the map before the Fourth of July, it surely is now."

"I don't like it," said C.J. "I haven't liked it ever since the *Reader's Digest* ran that story about me and our farming project. We don't need publicity, at least I don't. I'd rather be left alone. I think most of the vets would say the same thing."

"You know what, C.J.?"

"What?"

"I wouldn't be here if it wasn't for that *Reader's Digest* article. And neither would Pastor Vicki. Neither of us would be here."

He took Maggie's hands in his. "You are right," he said. "But I still don't like publicity. Talking about the press, I have a question for you."

"Yes," said Maggie.

"You told me about the Bible you found at the shooter's location as well as the scribbled 'Sinners Deserve to Die' note. Why didn't you or the sheriff mention those things to the press?"

"Couple of reasons. Had we mentioned it, the press would have been on Pastor Jacob like a plague of grasshoppers in a wheat field. He probably would've liked the publicity, but the members of his congregation don't deserve to be pulled through the mud, and that surely would have happened."

"But how do you know one of his church members didn't do it, didn't do all of the mean things that have been happening in Link Lake the last few months?" asked C.J., taking another sip of water.

"We don't know that," said Maggie. "But it's wrong to point fingers when you have no evidence."

"You have a point, Maggie. No pun intended."

"By the way, happy birthday," C.J. said rather sheepishly. He had intended to wish her a happy birthday when they first sat down at the table. "Here's to many more," he said as he raised his nearly empty water glass.

# 32

"So Fred, you recovered from the Fourth of July?" asked Oscar as he slid onto his chair at the Eat Well Café.

"It's gonna take a while, Oscar. It's gonna take a while. Who do you suppose was the shooter? Got any theories about that?"

"I really don't. The important point is that the shooter missed," said Oscar.

"You got that right."

"Sure put Link Lake on the map, though. Never saw so many TV trucks and newspaper people in this town. In my eighty years of rememberin' stuff, never saw anythin' like this. I suspect some folks have called this sort of outpourin' of interest by the press a media circus," said Oscar.

"Helluva way to be put on the map," said Fred. "I can see the headlines now: 'Come to Link Lake, the town where people shoot at U.S. senators.'"

"I don't know what to make of it. What has happened to our peaceful town? Church burnin', dogs bein' shot, grocery store trashed, church services disrupted, and now a shootin'. Where is all this hate comin' from?" mused Oscar, holding his coffee cup with both hands. "You know, Fred, I sometimes think I shouldn't have given those five acres of land to C.J. He came out of the military with but one good leg and a head full of hurt and anger. I really thought working the land would help him with his troubles—I guess it has. But since this group of disabled veterans moved here and started farming, and Pastor Vicki came here because she thought she could provide some help for these vets from another perspective, there's been nothin' but trouble."

"Oscar, I'd think you would be the last one to blame the disabled vets for what's happenin' in Link Lake," said Fred, looking his old friend in the eye.

"I'm not blamin' the vets, not at all. Good God, they need all the help they can get. No question about that. But I don't think Link Lake was ready for them, or that they were ready for Link Lake. Fred, we've got a bunch of folks here who want Link Lake to be just like it was fifty years ago. And we've got a handful of farmers like old John Wilson who think that unless you are milkin' at least a thousand cows, you ought not be farmin'. Two kinds of folks: those who don't want change and those who seem to be changin' in the wrong direction. I'm afraid some of these folks just can't wrap their minds around the fact that nothin' stays the same. Time marches on and things change. Even the weather is changin'. You keepin' up with this climate change thing, Fred?"

"Tryin' to, Oscar. But some people in this town think it's a hoax, dreamed up by some university professors lookin' for money to do research on something that doesn't exist."

"Oh, climate change is real. Just think of what's happenin' around the country. The floods, the droughts, the wildfires. All related to climate change. It's not comin' our way; it's already here," said Oscar, his brow wrinkling.

The two old men began working on their scrambled eggs, hash brown potatoes, and slices of thick bacon. Fred had read someplace that eating too many pancakes can cause you to gain weight and maybe affect your cholesterol as well.

"You know it's a funny thing," began Oscar.

"What's funny? Somebody spill his coffee?" said Fred.

"What's funny, Fred, is people here in Link Lake applaud John Wilson's decision to expand his dairy operation to a thousand cows and at the same time some of them turn up their noses at these disabled vets tryin' to farm on five or ten acres. Kind of ironic."

"I'm tryin' to follow your line of palaver, Oscar, but what in hell does ironic mean?" asked Fred.

"It means doin' or sayin' something different from what's expected," said Oscar.

"Well, why didn't you just say so?"

"Because ironic is the right word to describe what's goin' on in Link Lake, where a bunch of people are opposed to how the disabled veterans are farmin' with their focus on sellin' fresh fruit, vegetables, and meat products directly to customers. And they see what these vets are doin' as new and different and somehow threatenin' farmers like John Wilson. These are the same people who stand up and proclaim the virtues of how farmin' was done fifty years ago—like we used to do it, Fred. And in large measure, just like what these disabled vets are doin' today. It's ironic," said Oscar.

"I'd just say it's strange, Oscar. People do dumb things. We've done dumb things."

"Speak for yourself, Fred. Speak for yourself," said Oscar, smiling.

"How's that writin' class going?" asked Fred, changing the subject.

"We met for the third time last week. And have I been surprised," said Oscar.

"Surprised? What could possibly be surprisin' in a dull old writin' workshop?" asked Fred. "Sorry to say this, Oscar, but for me, the dullest, least interestin' thing in the world is scribblin' down words on paper."

"Here's what happened," said Oscar, choosing not to respond to his friend's comment. "At the session before this one, I gave them an assignment. I asked them to write about some event that changed their lives. I made no mention of the war wounds that each of them experienced, but I was hopin' at least one of them would write about that. Well, guess what? One of them did and that was my grandson, C.J. He told in great detail how it happened, how he eventually lost the lower part of one of his legs. When he finished, there wasn't a dry eye in the room, includin' mine."

"He did that?" asked Fred. "That takes lots of guts to share. Most vets don't want to talk about their war wounds and how they got them."

"That's true, but I learned from talkin' with Pastor Vicki that once disabled veterans begin talkin' about their disabilities and how they got them, the healin' becomes a lot easier. After C.J. told his story about how he lost his leg, everyone else in the workshop decided it was a safe enough place for them to tell their stories as well. And that's what they did. I tell you, those people who are down on these disabled vets and their approach to farmin' should hear these stories. I'll bet you my last dime that they would change their minds. But you know what, Fred?"

"What?"

"These vets are gonna share their stories. We're gonna collect them in a book and get it printed. Pastor Vicki's gonna help them with the editin' and findin' a printer. They've decided to call their book *The Disabled Veterans of Settlers Valley: Our Stories.*

"It worked out a lot better than I thought it would. Pastor Vicki was right. Sometimes writin' down and sharin' your story turns out to be much more powerful than it appears on the surface. I'm pretty darn proud of this group of scribblers. I really am. This was our last meetin'. We had a little literary celebration at the end of it," said Oscar.

"A literary celebration? What pray tell is a literary celebration?" asked Fred.

"Well, we drank some Link Lake Brewery beer, ate a few bratwursts, and continued tellin' stories," said Oscar with a straight face.

Fred laughed.

# 33

C.J. heard his cell phone ringing. He had kept an old-fashioned phone ring—not one of these fancy church bells ringing, or some pop performer trying to sing. He answered.

"It's Maggie," said the voice on the other end of the connection.

"What can I do for you?" C.J. asked. He hadn't seen Maggie for a couple of days. C.J. had been trying to jury-rig an irrigation system at his farm. Grandpa Oscar had suggested that he keep a weather record and each day write down the high and low temperatures and rainfall amounts as they occurred. This morning he had looked at his weather record and noted that daytime temperatures had been in the mid to high eighties every day for more than a month. He also wrote that rainfall that had been so abundant in May and in June had about disappeared. Since mid-June, C.J. had recorded but two-tenths of an inch of rain. His garden crops needed rain. Settlers Valley needed rain.

"Could you stop by today? I'm concerned about my crops," Maggie said.

"We all are, Maggie. I'll be there in a few minutes."

When C.J. arrived at Maggie's little farm, she immediately took him out to her garden. C.J. shook his head as he saw the bottom leaves of the sweet corn curled, with a few leaves already turning brown. The potato plants had stopped growing. The lettuce leaves were rolled. The squash and pumpkin plant leaves were curled.

"Garden needs water, Maggie. Your crops are suffering," said C.J., tugging at his black beard. He vaguely remembered talking to Maggie about the need for watering her garden. But so far the rains had come regularly and no watering was necessary. "Have you got any garden hose?"

"Maybe. I've not spent much time in the old pump house. It's filled with junk, plus a colony of bats and more mice than I want to know about."

Together, C.J. and Maggie dug through the history of the farm piled away in the old pump house. They found several rusty ten-gallon milk cans and a leather horse harness, now stiff and covered with mildew, and they saw several horseshoes hanging on nails. "Good luck here on out," C.J. said. "Grandpa Oscar swears by horseshoes for good luck. He's got one hanging over the outside door into the kitchen."

"I don't feel very lucky, what with my crops drying up," said Maggie, looking glummer than C.J. had ever seen her. Finally, they discovered a garden hose, green, stiff, and unusable. "Looks to me like the first garden hose ever invented." She tossed the old hose aside. "What do we do now?" she asked.

"Well, we drive to town and buy you some new hose. You need to water your vegetables before they completely quit growing and die," said C.J.

"Buy hose with what? My cookie jar is about empty. And my credit card is almost maxed out," said Maggie.

"Tell you what, Maggie. I've got an extra few hundred feet of garden hose you can borrow. I've also got an extra sprinkler head you can use," said C.J.

"You sure? Don't you need it?"

"I've got enough garden hose. Besides, that's what it means to be a neighbor. We help each other. Ask Grandpa Oscar about that sometime. He thinks too many people these days want to go it alone. They've forgotten how to be neighbors like it was when he was actively farming. This may sound a little corny, Maggie, but one of Grandpa Oscar's sayings is a bit of an expansion on what we all believe—as we take care of the land, it will take care of us. He adds, as we take care of our neighbors, they will take care of us."

C.J. drove back to his place, picked up the extra hose and sprinkler head, and returned to Maggie's farm. She was busy in the kitchen, preparing lunch for the two of them. "I didn't expect any lunch," C.J. said.

He laid out the hose, set up the sprinkler head, and turned on the water. The most recent occupants of the old farmhouse had put in a new submersible pump and pressure tank, so there was plenty of water. C.J. directed the water on the potatoes, having learned from his grandfather that of all the vegetable crops, potatoes were the most water-hungry.

As they sat eating their lunch of grilled cheese sandwiches, C.J. carefully explained to Maggie that she should move the sprinkler head every hour or so to make sure the entire potato crop was watered before watering the vining crops, which also seemed in danger of dying if they soon didn't get a drink.

"Thank you for doing this, C.J.," Maggie said, putting her hand on his. "You are wonderful."

"I don't know how wonderful I am, but you are welcome," said C.J.

"Have you heard any more about the pipeline's decision?" asked Maggie. "We are about at the end of July, and if I remember, they said they'd decide where they wanted to put that dreaded pipeline about now."

"Nope, haven't heard a thing. Not even a rumor. Often there's a bunch of rumors about these things. Not this time."

"When's this country going to decide that the future is not more petroleum? Don't these people know about renewable energy?" said Maggie, who busied herself clearing the table of leftover lunch makings.

"I suspect they do. But the oil companies have a pile of money invested in getting the petroleum out of the ground and to the refineries. The refineries also have a lot of money invested in making gasoline and a hundred other products that are petroleum based. It becomes difficult to break the cycle. Change is tough. Always has been. Always will be," said C.J. as he got up from his chair.

"Kind of gloomy and doomy today," Maggie said, smiling.

"I suppose," said C.J., rubbing his beard.

"Coming over tonight?" Maggie asked, taking C.J.'s hand.

# 34

"You had a visitor yesterday, Fred?" asked Oscar as he tossed his John Deere cap on a chair and reached for the cup of coffee that stood in front of him.

"Yup, I did," Fred answered. "Guy from the Al-Mid Pipeline Company. Said his name was Emory something."

"Emory Sage," said Oscar.

"Yeah, Emory Sage. How'd you know?"

"Same fellow came to my place. Guess Al-Mid's made up its mind about where they want to dig in their pipeline. Kept the final decision under their hats. Still, haven't heard any official announcement," said Oscar.

"What'd the guy want?"

"Well, first I must say this Sage fellow seems like a decent sort. Not one of those high and mighty city-educated types that want you to believe that you are stupid and he is the only person who knows anything. There're folks like that around, you know. Overeducated types," said Oscar.

"What'd he have to say?"

"To start off, he didn't say much of anything. Talked a little about the weather. Said he liked the looks of my barn. I told him we'd cleaned it up some and that we are holdin' church services there until the church that burned was rebuilt. He found that kind of interestin'. I knew what the guy was doin'. He was tryin' to soften me up. I suspect he'd done a little checkin' and learned that I didn't think much of a pipeline snakin' across my farm. I figure he knew that from the way he was tryin' to be a decent sort, so I wouldn't end up yellin' at him and sendin' him skedaddlin' off my property," said Oscar.

"Did he get around to talkin' about easements and how much money you'd get from havin' the pipeline cross your farm?" asked Fred.

"Yeah, he did mention easements. I asked him what that amounted to. He left me with some papers to read. Said the written stuff had all I needed to know and if I had any questions, I should give him a call. He didn't get into much detail. Just that he was lookin' forward to workin' with me. He then kind of overdid it, I'd say," said Oscar.

"How so?"

"Well, he ended up throwin' me this compliment. Tellin' me what an upstandin' citizen I was by givin' land to my grandson who was a disabled veteran. Tellin' me how great it was that I, in my eighties, was helpin' the disabled veterans learn somethin' about farmin' as they try to overcome their disabilities," said Oscar.

"How'd he know all that stuff? Sounds a little weird to me," said Fred.

"I've been thinkin' about all this. Wonderin' if on the one hand the guy had really done his homework and wants me to know that he is well aware of the goings-on in Settlers Valley, or on the other hand, somethin' funny is goin' on. Somethin' just didn't seem right about this guy. I can't put my finger on it. On the one hand, he seemed down to earth, ordinary, and knowledgeable. But on the other, he represents the Al-Mid Pipeline Company. Somewhere I read that the Al-Mid will do whatever it takes to lay their pipeline where they want to lay it."

"You know, Oscar, that's almost exactly what the guy did when he stopped at my place. Butterin' me up about how good my buildings look, thankin' me for helpin' these disabled vets learn about farmin'.

147

I've met people like this before. I try not to let it show, but my BS indicator kicks in, and it surely did with this guy. I suspect he left me with a packet of written stuff same as you got. Say, do you suppose he stopped at each of the disabled vets' farms as well?" asked Fred.

"I bet he did. I haven't talked with C.J. today. But I would guess he worked his way all across the valley the last few days. Wonder what kind of soft talk he gave the vets. The guy is a smooth one. He surely is," said Oscar.

"So what're we gonna do about all this? Just let the pipeline guys put in that dirty old pipeline or raise a little hell about it? Maybe a lot of hell. We don't need no damn pipeline messin' up our farms and screwin' up what the disabled vets are trying to accomplish. We sure don't," said Fred. His face was getting red as his anger began to show.

"I'll talk with C.J. this afternoon. See what he thinks we should do. What I know for sure is I'm not gonna sit on my hands, sign some damn lease, and try to live with a pipeline on my farm," said Oscar, raising his voice so that a couple sitting at a nearby table looked in his direction.

# 35

That afternoon Oscar drove over to C.J.'s place. "Did a guy from the pipeline company stop by here yesterday?" asked Oscar.

"Sure did. Real smooth character. Tried to tell me what a great job I'm doing in helping other disabled vets. Real smooth. But you know, Grandpa, I've been around the tree a couple of times in my life, and I could see through that guy like he had a window in his head. I knew exactly what he was doing. I tried not to let on, to see if he'd dig himself into a verbal hole. But he didn't. The guy has obviously been doing this for a while. He's good. I'll give him credit for that," said C.J.

"The same guy stopped by my place," said Oscar. "Same approach. Tellin' me what a great guy I am and what wonderful things I'm doin'. The guy was filled with BS, but I suppose if your job is to tell people how great it is to have a pipeline dug into your farm, this is one way to do it. I didn't argue with the guy. Didn't have a chance. He did all the talkin'. So, what's next?"

"I don't know," said C.J. "What I got from this guy was the pipeline is hell-bent on coming across Settlers Valley and we'd better accept it. I was so damn mad I felt like choking the guy, but I tried to stay calm. And I mostly did. But you know what, Grandpa, there's something shady going on."

"Lots of shady goin' on," Oscar said.

"I don't trust this pipeline company one bit," said C.J. "Not one bit. I'm driving over to Maggie's place to find out what she knows."

When he arrived at Maggie's farm, C.J. parked his pickup in his usual place. He glimpsed Maggie working in her garden, moving the garden hose and the watering head that was keeping her vegetables alive but just barely. She waved when she saw C.J. and Lucky. "Hi, C.J.," she yelled.

C.J. walked out into Maggie's garden. It looked better than it had before she started her watering regime, but the plants were far behind how they would appear if they had sufficient water. With the hose and watering head placed where she wanted them, Maggie brushed away the bubbles of sweat on her forehead with a big red handkerchief she always had in her pocket.

"What's up?" she asked, smiling broadly as she petted Lucky. She and C.J. had been getting along well, not only sharing her bed but carrying on extended conversations about everything from her take on the politics of the day to her views on religion—topics that many people avoided.

"Did you have a visitor from the pipeline company yesterday?" C.J. asked.

"I did. I looked out and saw this guy with a clipboard walking in my sweet corn patch. The fellow never stopped at the house, never asked for any kind of permission to walk on my property. He was just there. When I asked him why he was trespassing on my farm, he just smiled. He told me his name, which I've forgotten. Said he was an engineer with the Al-Mid Pipeline Company.

"I quietly told him, 'People around here ask permission before they go traipsing through other people's sweet corn fields.' He said he already had permission. I told him I didn't think so and the guy left. He said he'd be back, with the sheriff if necessary," Maggie said.

"What the hell was that all about?" C.J. asked.

"Beats me. But something strange is going on. Has the Al-Mid Pipe Line Company decided to try and build their pipeline here in Settlers Valley without telling anybody?"

"Strange, strange," said C.J., rubbing his beard. "The engineer guy didn't show up at my place, another guy did. The guy was trying to get me to sign a lease giving the company permission to build on my farm. The same guy talked to Grandpa Oscar and Fred Russo."

"Okay, so the pipeline company has its eye on Settlers Valley. What I don't get is why was this engineer guy smugly walking in my cornfield, while you get another guy trying to have you sign a lease," mused Maggie, shifting to remembering her training as a detective in the military police. "Tell you what, C.J. You and Lucky sit yourselves down under that shade tree over there while I make a few phone calls."

C.J. wondered who she was calling. He thought, *Is there some kind of conspiracy going on with this pipeline company?*

In a few minutes, Maggie was back. "I called some of our fellow Back to the Land farmers. Not one of them had a visitor from the pipeline company. When I told them about the pipeline's decision to build here in the valley, they were as surprised as I was when you told me. And to a person, they are mad as hell and wondering what's going to happen next. Frankly, I'm worried."

"So what are we going to do?" asked C J., once more running his hand through his beard.

"Pretty damn clear to me," said Maggie. Her face was now red and she was opening and closing her fists. "I'm going to organize a protest and you, C.J., are going to help me. If these birds think they are dealing with some namby-pamby disabled vets—well, they are going to wish they never tangled with us."

C.J. had not seen this side of Maggie before. "What . . . what do you want me to do?" he asked.

"Well, first you call a meeting of all the disabled vet families, where you tell them what's going on and you discuss how we can block these bastards," said Maggie. This was the first time C.J. had heard Maggie curse so much. "While you are doing that, I'm going to sit down at my computer and put together a social media protest that's going to curl the hair of those pipeline lackeys."

"You . . . you sure you want do that?" asked C.J.

"You bet I'm sure, never more sure of anything. These pipeline people sneaking around trying to put one over on our disabled veterans group, well, it's downright despicable."

"But doesn't that mean we'll get a bunch of outsiders rolling into Link Lake, professional protestor types, who'll destroy any goodwill we've been building with the locals here? Some of the locals aren't too happy with our group right now. Remember what happened on the Fourth of July?"

"I have not forgotten what happened on the Fourth of July. The sheriff and I are still trying to figure all that out. One day we'll know. It just takes time to put all the pieces together."

"I don't know, Maggie. This protesting on social media can backfire on us," said C.J.

"So you don't think I should do it?"

"Yeah, I guess that's what I'm saying," said C.J., now wondering where this conversation was going.

"Well, C.J.," said Maggie. She was standing right in front of him and shaking her finger in his face. "I don't care what you think. I'm going to do it. People need to know about this oil company and their devious strategies."

C.J. turned, and he and Lucky walked toward his pickup. C.J. was shaking his head. *What now?* he thought. *Is it over between Maggie and me just because of this damn pipeline?*

# 36

C.J., smarting from the argument he had with Maggie, nonetheless got busy organizing a meeting of all the Back to the Land Veterans and anyone else who wanted an update on the pipeline company's plans. C.J. made sure that Pastor Vicki would be there and asked her if she would do a little research on the civil rights protests of the 1960s and 1970s, especially those led by Dr. Martin Luther King Jr., who was committed to nonviolence. He promoted the meeting as an opportunity for persons interested in learning more about the Al-Mid Pipeline Company and their plans for building a pipeline in the valley, making no mention of planning a protest. C.J. thought, *If the pipeline company can be devious, so can I.* He asked the pipeline company to send a representative, but they declined.

It was a warm night in late July, and Oscar's barn was nearly filled with people. The temperature had been in the low nineties every day for almost two weeks, and it was stiflingly hot in the barn. Every farmer in the area had suffered from the dry weather and had been hoping and praying for rain. But there was no rain. Every evening, old-time farmers Oscar Anderson and Fred Russo looked to the west at sunset, searching for a hint of what might be a coming rainstorm. But they saw nothing. No sign of rain.

All the disabled vets and their spouses and children were at the meeting. C.J. wondered if Maggie would show up after their argument. But she was there, arriving late and sitting in the back with notebook in hand. Oscar and Fred were there, along with a handful of other farmers in the valley, including John and Florence Wilson, who had the largest farm in the valley with a thousand acres and soon a thousand milk cows.

C.J. figured that Wilson would argue for the pipeline. He wondered how Wilson would react when he discovered that the Back to the Land Veterans were unanimous in their disapproval.

C.J. opened the meeting. "Thank you for coming out on this stifling hot evening. We sure could use some rain, but we're not here to talk about the weather because there is nothing we can do about it. We can do something about the oil company that has decided to bury its pipe straight across our farms. We can show the pipeline people we don't want them messing up our land."

A round of applause followed. C.J. glanced at the Wilsons. He and his wife were not applauding. They did not look happy. "Before getting to the formal part of the meeting, I'd like to do a little checking. How many of you have had a fellow by the name of Emory Sage, a representative of the Al-Mid Pipeline Company, stop by your farm to talk about a lease for the pipeline to cross your land?"

C.J. held up his hand, as did his grandfather, Fred Russo, and John Wilson. Except for C.J., none of the Back to the Land Veterans members did. C.J. asked a second question. "How many of you had someone from the pipeline company appear on your land and claim they had permission to be there?" All the veterans held up their hands. C.J. glanced toward Maggie in the back of the room. She was writing in her notebook. Part of C.J. wanted to inquire about why this was, why the fellow with the lease information stopped by some of the farms and not others. And why some veterans saw pipeline people on their property without asking for permission. But he didn't.

C.J. continued. "I asked the pipeline company to send a representative to this meeting, but they declined. I wanted them to give us some details of what they have in mind. I did a little digging myself. The company wants about a thirty-foot-wide permanent easement on each of the farms where the pipeline plans to run. They also want another twenty-foot additional easement for what they call their 'construction activities.' After they have installed the pipeline, the temporary construction easement ends. The permanent easement lasts until either the pipeline is abandoned or the company releases the easement. Any questions about the easement situation?"

Ben Rostom, who raised free-range chickens, held up his hand. Rostom, tall and thin and deeply tanned from working outside, had lost part of one arm in the war.

"Yes, Ben."

"Nobody from the pipeline company has talked to me about an easement. I talked to the fellow I caught walking in my chicken yard the other day. He said he was an engineer with the pipeline company and he acted as if he already had permission and that I had already signed an easement with the company. What's that all about?" asked Ben.

"I don't know," said C.J. "From the number of hands I saw up a couple minutes ago, you're not the only one with a trespasser on your property. I'll do some more digging."

"What's the size of pipe they plan to lay, and, just because I'm curious, how many barrels of this crude oil that they're digging for in Canada do they plan to ship our way," asked Kari Detrick, who raised pasture-fed hogs.

"Well, let's see if I can find that information in my notes, Kari," said C.J. as he thumbed through a little pile of papers he had in front of him. "Here it is. They say the pipeline's going to be thirty-six inches in diameter and will transport about four hundred thousand barrels a day. Any more questions?"

Fred Russo's hand was up.

"Yes, Fred."

"C.J., what do we know about pipeline leaks? Should we be concerned about that?"

"You've read about the Keystone pipeline that runs from Canada through the Dakotas and south where it connects with another pipeline. Well, Keystone had thirty-five leaks and spills in its first year of operation. Spills are always a possibility. One more thing I read recently. Tar sands oil is considered the most polluting kind of oil. In addition to being highly corrosive because of all the sulfur and other chemicals in it, when there is a spill, it is especially difficult to clean up. It's heavy, and it sinks to the bottom of water. Any other questions? Anyone else have a comment before we move on?" asked C.J.

John Wilson's hand shot up. "Yes, I have something," Wilson said as he walked to the podium.

"First, it's clear to me that you folks don't favor this pipeline comin' to our valley. I've been here a lot longer than most of you, except for my old farmer friends, Oscar Anderson and Fred Russo. Times are changin'. Farming is changin'. As much as we want to not believe it, we do need oil to farm. I must say, and this is no exaggeration, we need oil to live."

C.J. wondered how long Wilson would go on. C.J. wanted to get into some of the specifics of how to prevent this oil company from ever building here.

"The building of this pipeline in Settlers Valley is more than a local happenin'. Our country needs to produce more energy so we can compete in the global market. Pipelines are the most inexpensive way to do that. C.J. was talkin' about oil spills. He didn't mention how many trains carryin' crude oil have derailed and spilled their contents, how many river barges carryin' crude oil have had spills. This country obviously needs to wean itself from Middle East oil, and it needs to do that in the most efficient and safest way possible. I look forward to havin' this new pipeline crossing my farm. Welcomin' the pipeline to Settlers Valley is the most patriotic thing we can do," said Wilson, and he turned and walked back to his seat. The crowd was quiet. No clapping, no hissing, just quiet.

"Thank you," C.J. said. "Any other questions or comments?" He paused. "Okay, let's move on. I've asked Pastor Vicki to do a little research in preparation for this meeting. Pastor Vicki, the floor is yours."

"Thanks, C.J. C.J. asked me talk about how we can protest the coming of this pipeline in a nonviolent way."

Upon hearing these words, John Wilson jumped to his feet and yelled, "Why in the hell do you want to protest the comin' of the pipeline? Didn't you hear what I just said? You'll all be sorry for doin' this." His face was red and the veins in his neck were throbbing. "You will pay for this," he yelled as he and his wife stalked out of the barn.

"Well, I guess we know where John Wilson stands," said Pastor Vicki before she began talking about Martin Luther King Jr. and his approach to nonviolent protests during the civil rights marches from the mid-1950s to the late 1960s.

# 37

*Ames County Argus*

AL-MID PIPELINE MAKES DECISION

The *Argus* has learned that the Al-Mid Pipeline Company has selected Settlers Valley as the site for its new pipeline. Although it has made no formal announcement, the company has begun discussing leases with landowners in the valley, the first indication that Settlers Valley will be the site for their operation. Emory Sage, field representative for the pipeline company, said, "We discussed all the alternatives, and we landed on two possibilities here in Ames County. Settlers Valley quickly beat out the other site for several reasons. Building in the river valley will save the company considerable money on both the engineering and construction phases of the project. The area is relatively flat, and although we realize we'll be constructing across both large and small land holdings and crossing Settlers Creek at several places, we believe these landholders will quickly embrace this new, modern pipeline with its potential for helping the U.S. cut its dependency on Mideastern oil.

When the *Argus* asked about the potential for pushback from the landholders, notably the Back to the Land Veterans, Sage said, "Several of the vets have expressed their opposition to the pipeline crossing their lands, but they may not realize that we already have their permission. John Wilson, the most significant landowner in the valley, is four-square behind the pipeline and looks forward to having it crossing his large farm. Some of the retired farmers haven't come around to accepting the pipeline, but when they learn all the facts, I believe they'll approve of the project. The Al-Mid Pipeline Company would like to thank all the citizens of Ames County and especially the landowners in Settlers Valley for their acceptance and in several instances, enthusiastic embracing of this new, modern and abundantly safe pipeline.

Oscar Anderson angrily tossed his cap on a nearby chair and sat down, facing his old friend, Fred.

"What're you so steamed up about this morning?" asked Fred.

"Did you read this issue of the *Argus*, Fred?" Oscar asked as he tossed the newspaper on the table in front of him.

Fred glanced at the date on the paper. "Nope, it's on my reading agenda, though. Probably get at it this afternoon."

"Well, you'd better take time to read this story right now, Fred," said Oscar as he stabbed his finger at the story on the front page.

"Okay, I'll read it. Settle down, Oscar, or you'll have a heart attack," said Fred as he adjusted his glasses and began reading.

"Coffee, Oscar, Fred?" the waitress asked with coffee cups and coffee pot in hand.

"Sure," said Oscar. Fred nodded as he continued reading the front-page story. Oscar, sipping his coffee, watched his friend as he read.

"Well," said Fred as he handed the paper back to Oscar.

"Well, what?" asked Oscar.

"Well, it's quite a story, with a lot of stuff I didn't know about. I didn't know the vets have given permission to the pipeline to build across their farms. Why would they be protestin' if they'd already signed the leases givin' permission to the pipeline company to build?" asked Fred.

"The article didn't say they signed leases, only said they had already given permission for the pipeline to cross their land," said Oscar.

"How could they do that?" said Fred.

"I don't know, Fred. That Sage guy is lyin' through his teeth. I'm guessin' the only person signin' a lease is John Wilson. I'll bet you a dime to a dollar that he's the only damn one. The only one."

"You'd think the paper would have done a little checkin' to see if this Sage fellow was tellin' the truth or just blowin' smoke," said Fred.

"You know why they didn't do any fact-checkin'? You know why, Fred?"

"Not a clue."

"Turn to the next page in the paper," instructed Oscar.

Fred put down his cup, picked up the paper once more, and turned to page 2, which was a full-page ad.

"That's quite an ad," said Fred. "But what a lie. I'm no friend of that damn pipeline company, and from what I heard at the meetin' in your barn the other night, none of the veterans in the valley are much taken with the idea either. I talked with my old buddy Joe Berry over at the school. He said nobody is madder about all this pipeline talk than Principal Lucy James. She told Joe that this Sage guy stopped by her office with one of these draft leases in his hand. After he told her about how the pipeline had plans to cut right through the school forest, includin' them needin' to tear down their new shelter, she about blew her stack. Joe happened to be walkin' by her office at the time. He said you could hear her way out in the hall, reamin' out this guy without mercy. Joe said he saw the Sage fellow leave. The guy walked out of the school with his tail between his legs. Imagine when she reads this stuff in the paper. Sage makes it sound that all is hunky-dory in Settlers Valley. And we're huggin' this pipeline idea like some long-lost friend has just come back to town."

"Somethin' damn fishy is goin' on, Fred," Oscar said. "I know for a fact that C.J. has not signed a lease for the pipeline to go through his property, and yet this Sage guy says he has permission from the disabled vets. Somethin' goofy here. That's for damn sure."

"So whatta you gonna do, Oscar?"

"Well, the first thing I'm gonna do is stick one of those big red No Pipeline signs out by the road so that everybody that drives by will see it and know where I stand. Next thing, I'm gonna talk with C.J. to see if he's heard anything. The disabled vets must be furious, readin' that they'd given permission to somethin' that they hadn't. Article shoots a big hole in our effort to protest. People will think we're a bunch of country loonies, protestin' somethin' that we've already agreed should happen."

# 38

When Oscar returned home from the Eat Well, he saw C.J.'s pickup parked by the house. C.J. was standing by the vehicle, holding a copy of the *Argus*.

"What in the hell is this?" said C.J., tugging on his beard. "Did you read this?" he asked as he approached Oscar, who had just gotten out of his car. "This is a pack of lies. Bald-faced lies." He slapped the folded paper against his hand.

"Hold on there, C.J. Yes, I've read it, and I'm as mad as you are. Maybe even madder," said Oscar as he walked over to his grandson.

"What's got into this pipeline guy? He makes it sound like the pipeline is a done deal. Hell, we haven't started to tell that pipeline company where they can shove their damn oil pipe," said C.J., who was red in the face. "Grandpa, I've been pretty angry with Maggie— we haven't talked in more than a week. She wanted to use social media to tell the world what the pipeline people had planned for the Back to the Land Veterans. Wanted to share our plight on the internet. I told her not to do it, and she did it anyway. Made me kind of mad. I didn't want a bunch of people feeling sorry for us and, worse yet, coming to Settlers Valley to help us protest."

"I noticed that you two haven't spent any time together lately. I did notice that," said Oscar.

"You know what, Grandpa? Maggie was right. Something's going on here that's bigger than us. This smells bad, Grandpa. Something downright awful is going on. I'll bet my pickup on it. And Maggie's idea of creating a website for our group and using social networks to help our cause is probably what we need right now."

"So you gonna tell Maggie she was right?"

"I will, I will," said C.J. "She is one smart woman."

C.J. punched the numbers into his cell phone for Maggie. He heard the phone ring four times. He wondered if she was still so angry with him that she would not pick up. And then he heard a quiet voice answer, "This is Maggie."

"How are you?" C.J. asked, not really knowing how to start the conversation.

"I've been better," said Maggie.

"Is there . . ." C.J. hesitated. "Is there any possibility that Lucky and I could stop by to see you?"

Silence. C.J. wondered if she had hung up.

"That would be okay," said Maggie. And then C.J. had to strain to hear, "I've missed you, C.J."

"I'll be there in five minutes," C.J. said, stuffing his cell phone in his pocket, whistling for Lucky, and climbing into his pickup.

Driving into Maggie's yard, he saw her standing on the porch of the old farmhouse. C.J. had almost forgotten how beautiful she was and thought how stupid he had been to march off in a huff over something that he now realized might help solve the enormous problem now facing all the Back to the Land Veterans farming in Settlers Valley.

When C J walked up to her, he saw that her eyes were red. She had been crying. She rushed up to C.J. and embraced him. She stepped back and said, "I'm so glad to see you," holding both of his hands in hers and looking into his eyes.

"I'm sort of here on business," C.J. muttered. "Did you read the last issue of the *Argus*?"

"I did," said Maggie, regaining her composure as she wiped her eyes with C.J.'s big red handkerchief that he handed her. "I read it this morning, and I've been busy developing a website for the vets here in the valley. I know you don't approve, but C.J., we need all the help we can get if we are going to beat back this pipeline."

"Maggie, you are one hundred percent right about doing this. I was wrong. Dead wrong. I guess I figured that if we vets got together along with Pastor Vicki, my grandpa, and Fred Russo, we could send the pipeline packing. The *Argus* article makes it sound like a done deal. Did you know that the pipeline wants to run all the way through the school forest, including demolishing the shelter house that the school just built?"

"I didn't know about the school forest," said Maggie. "But I'm sure Lucy James also knows about the eminent domain laws that the pipeline will surely use to get places like the school to allow the pipeline on their property."

"I sure hope your social media message works. We need money to fight this pipeline. What little money we had went toward producing a few No Pipeline signs. We need to get on TV and radio with our message. We need to buy ads in newspapers," C.J. said as he ran his hands through his beard.

"I read the piece in the *Argus* a couple of times, C.J. Either this Emory Sage guy is lying about permissions and leases, or he knows something the rest of us don't know. I'll start doing a little digging. I've got friends in Washington who can help," said Maggie.

"We're going to need all the help we can get. By the way, have you and the sheriff gotten any further figuring out who's been raising hell here in the valley?" C.J. asked.

"We've sent the rifle and shell casing to the crime lab in Madison, but no word back yet. We're assuming all the events are related, but there's also the possibility that they are not, that several different people are involved. This community has really torn itself apart. I've always hung my hat on the word 'hope.' This community seems to be thriving on hate," said Maggie.

"You've got that right," said C.J.

"Can you stay for lunch?" Maggie asked. "I've got some great dessert on the menu." She smiled.

# 39

It was a week after C.J. met with Maggie that he drove into Link Lake on his way to the grocery store for some basics. The valley had gotten about a tenth of an inch of rain, not enough to break the near summer-long drought but enough to keep the farmers in the valley from losing their crops. By watering his garden, C.J. continued to have a reasonable crop of vegetables both for sale and for his own eating. C.J. had a small load of produce he was delivering to the grocery cooperative. He also needed some meat. He especially enjoyed the distinctive flavor of the free-range broilers that Ben Rostom raised. Driving by the site of the Link Lake People's Church, C.J. saw the new church building rising from the ashes. He stopped when he glimpsed Pastor Vicki, who was watching the builders work.

"C.J., good to see you. What brings you to town?" Pastor Vicki asked.

"Delivering some vegetables to the grocery co-op and doing a little shopping."

"Expect the drought is hitting you like your fellow vets in the valley," said Pastor Vicki.

"I'm told you have a straight line to the big guy in charge of the weather," C.J. said, pointing upward.

"I wish," said Pastor Vicki. "It'd be raining if I did. I understand this pipeline thing is coming to a head. From what I read in the paper they are about ready to build."

"They may think so, but my fellow vets and I have a different idea. Did you see the new website Maggie put together for us?"

"I did. It's pretty impressive," said Pastor Vicki. "I talked to Maggie yesterday."

"Did she tell you that her little video of several vets got a thousand responses in just three days? And don't tell anyone, but so far people have donated more than five thousand dollars, with more coming in each day. We're putting ads in the local and regional papers, buying time on several TV and radio stations, and making a bunch of signs," said C.J.

"Almost sounds like a David and Goliath thing. Those pipeline companies have lots of money," said Pastor Vicki.

"How many people do you think will turn out for the protest parade at the company's offices in Minneapolis this weekend? Maggie said that you did most of the organizing and the two of you will be traveling to the Twin Cities to lead it all," said C.J.

"Looks like about a thousand people will be marching, letting everyone in that part of the country know that a group of disabled vets doesn't plan on rolling over for the heavy-handed antics of the Al-Mid Pipeline Company."

"Thanks for your all your help, Vicki."

"Know what else is happening? Not only are veterans from around the country on your side, but we've touched a nerve with several environmental groups, both in this country and Canada, that are opposed to digging up thousands of acres of pristine forest land for some very low-quality petroleum," said Pastor Vicki. "I've also talked with several people, mostly veterans, who said that when we find out where and when the pipeline company is digging in their first pipes, they will come, protest, and make it more than a little difficult for them to work."

"I hope this hard work pays off. The drought is about to do us all in. The last thing we need is a pipeline to add to our misery," said C.J.

Arriving at the grocery cooperative, C.J. struck up a conversation with Tommy Green. "How's it going, Tommy?"

"Not so good. Drought has been raising havoc with the valley's vegetable crop. But we vets are a tough bunch. Any word on when it'll rain?"

"Nope," said C.J. "Grandpa Oscar usually knows when rain is on the way. I asked him the other day, and he shook his head. If Oscar doesn't know when it's gonna rain, nobody knows."

Just then Ben Rostom walked in, carrying a big box that he sat on the counter near the cash register. "Here's ten more broilers for you, Tommy," Ben said.

"Good to see you, Ben," C.J. said, extending his hand. "You making it through the drought?"

"Just barely. Pasture for my chickens is looking pretty thin, some of it is just about dried up. We don't get some rain in a week or so, I don't know what I'll do," said Ben.

"I guess everybody in the valley is praying for rain," C.J. said. "I suspect you hear this often, Ben, but those broilers you are raising are just the best. I can't remember when I ever tasted anything better. I bought one here last week. Put it on the grill, and, well, it was wonderful. Reminded me of when I was a kid and had Sunday chicken dinner at Grandpa Oscar's place."

"Thank you, C.J. Always good to hear from someone who appreciates hard work, as I know you do. The problem these days is city folks look at the price of something ahead of its quality. Too bad. Those of us raising pasture-fed chickens have to charge a little more. I hope we can get more folks appreciating quality in their food."

"How right you are, Ben. It's the same thing with vegetables. It's hard to believe, but lots of people drive by our little grocery cooperative featuring homegrown vegetables for the big chain grocery where the vegetables are grown on large industrial farms many miles from here. Just because the vegetables are a few cents cheaper," said C.J.

As C.J. drove home later, his mind was churning with the discussion he had with Ben Rostom and Tommy Green. *The big challenge we Back to the Land types face is how to help consumers understand why quality should be more important than price, especially when it comes to food*, thought C.J. as he drove past pastures that had been green in early June but were now brown and desertlike in appearance.

He thought about all that had happened so far this year. These months surely were the toughest so far for the Back to the Land Veterans. *One challenge after the other. Somebody is just plain mad at us—members of the Church of the Holy Redeemed, perhaps? Their pastor is livid that we disabled vets are supporting the Link Lake People's Church. Then there is the Eagle Party. John Wilson is no friend of our veterans' group and no friend of how we farm. Could someone in the Eagle Party have burned down the church and committed the other skullduggery that has gone on in Link Lake and in Settlers Valley? Are several people behind all of this mean stuff going on, or just one person? And then the pipeline, the dreaded pipeline coming through the valley has everybody mad as hell. And put on top of it all the weather, no rain for weeks. What more could happen to us?*

# 40

Upon returning home, C.J. grabbed up his favorite garden hoe and headed to his garden. Something always needed hoeing. Even during dry weather, when the vegetables struggled to stay alive, the weeds kept growing. C.J. wondered when the plant breeders developing new vegetable varieties would get around to looking at the weeds that seemed to thrive whether it was wet or dry. He had been reading some of the research reports on climate change. It seemed clear that Wisconsin and indeed much of the nation would see changes in weather patterns caused by the broader effects of climate change. Drought, like this one central Wisconsin was experiencing, will come more often. Heavy rains would likely also occur, sometimes even at flood levels.

But right now, in late July, C.J. scanned the sky to the west looking for clouds suggesting rain might be coming. He saw nothing. Just a blazing hot sun in a bright-blue sky. There was no wind, not like the previous days, when a hot, dry wind blew from the southwest, generating clouds of dust picked up from the massive open vegetable fields that large-scale farmers were growing a few miles west of Link Lake. Grandpa Oscar told C.J. that those dusty days had reminded him of the 1930s, during the Great Depression, when much of Ames County's cultivated fields felt the wrath of no rain and hot winds. Tons of fertile topsoil had left the area in dirty-brown clouds.

As C.J. hoed, he reminded himself of why he and his fellow vets were farming on small plots, often surrounded by trees, so that the searing hot winds resulted in no soil erosion. But the hot winds still caused the vegetable crops to quit growing. Even with C.J.'s daily watering, his plants were merely surviving. Everything needed rain.

That night C.J. heard it again. The wind. The hot wind had picked up once more and tore at C.J.'s cabin, making sleeping difficult. It had a menacing, mean sound. C.J. thought once more of the open fields to the west of Settlers Valley, and the dust that on bad days had nearly obscured the sun.

At 6:00 a.m. C.J. sat on his porch, listening to the wind tearing across the valley, watching the sun trying to shine through a brownish cloud of dust. He talked to Lucky, who sat beside him.

"We gonna have any luck today, Lucky, or is this another of those downer days like we've been having lately?" he asked.

The big dog looked up with an expression that seemed to say that he understood some of the anxiety his master was feeling. C.J.'s phone rang.

"It's Ben Rostom," C.J. heard upon answering.

"You're up bright and early," C.J. said. "What can I do for you?"

"Could you come over, C.J.? Something awful has happened. Just awful."

"I'll be right there," said C.J. "Watch over things, Lucky," he said as he stuffed his phone into his pocket and hurried out to his pickup.

C.J. saw Ben Rostom standing by one of his broiler houses. The building was designed so he could move it every few days so the broilers would have fresh grass to eat.

"Over here, C.J.," Ben said, motioning to C.J. as he climbed out of his pickup.

"Morning, Ben," said C.J.

"Thanks for coming, C.J. Look in here," Ben held open the door to the little broiler house.

"Good God, what happened?" said C.J. as he saw dead and bleeding broilers scattered around the wooden floor.

"I counted twenty-five of them dead," said Ben. "Twenty-five broilers that I was gonna take to the processing plant today. All dead." He was holding his prosthetic right arm with his good left arm.

"Do you think some weasel got in here and did this, or maybe a fox?" asked Ben. "I did a count, and two broilers are missing. I haven't looked real close. Just too much blood and gore for me to handle this early in the morning."

"Don't believe an animal did this," said C.J. "An animal wouldn't slit each broiler's throat. Somebody with a big sharp knife did this. Ben, you should call the sheriff."

"Who in the hell would do this, C.J.? Who in the hell is that mean?"

"I wish I knew, Ben. I wish I knew."

Ben immediately called the sheriff's office. C.J. called Maggie, to see if she could come over and give her take on the carnage. When he told her what had happened, Maggie said, "Don't touch anything, and don't move anything. Just leave it as you first saw it."

As C.J. and Ben waited for the arrival of the sheriff and Maggie, they stood by the broiler house, not saying much of anything. C.J. was thinking, *Was what happened here related to all the other stuff that's been going on in the valley?* This situation seemed a bit different. A lot of lives were lost here, even if they were only chicken lives.

Maggie arrived first, looked in the broiler house, and then said, "What a mess. I'm sorry, Ben. This is awful."

"Thanks," said Ben. He looked close to tears. "I've just begun to take in a little money with the sale of these broilers, and now this had to happen."

"You'll make it, Ben," said Maggie, giving him a big hug.

With lights flashing on his squad, the sheriff drove into the yard and quickly walked toward where C.J., Ben, and Maggie were standing. "So what have we got here?" asked the sheriff.

"Take a look," said C.J., pointing to the open door.

"What a mess," said the sheriff. "Any idea what or who did this?"

"Well, we've ruled out an animal," offered C.J. "That's why we called you."

"What's your take on this, Maggie? You find anything?"

"Not yet, just got here a few minutes before you did," Maggie said.

Grabbing a stick that stood leaning against the building, the sheriff began poking around the carcasses of the dead broilers, trying to avoid fresh blood splattered on the walls and on the wooden floor.

"Wait, what have we here?" the sheriff said as he moved a broiler carcass aside with the stick. "Look at this."

C.J., Ben, and Maggie looked through the open window and saw the sheriff pointing.

"Can you see this?" he asked. "It's a footprint in the blood. Whoever did this left us a clue. Now we know that the person who killed these chickens was a man or a woman with big feet, and we know something about the kind of shoes they were wearing." The sheriff pulled his cell phone from his pocket and began taking pictures of the footprint as well as the rest of the crime scene.

"Here's what I'm wondering," mused the sheriff. "Is this the same guy that's been harassing this community starting with the burning of the church?" He left the question hanging in the air. "I wonder if this has anything to do with you folks not wanting the pipeline to cross your property? Just asking."

# 41

Six thirty, Monday morning. C.J. and Lucky sat on his porch that looked out over his vegetable gardens, Settlers Creek, and the valley beyond. Since the drought, C.J. had noticed that the flow of Settlers Creek had diminished a bit, though not as much as he would have expected considering how dry it was. He was aware of the amount of water the nearby large-scale vegetable farmers were pouring on their thousands of acres of sweet corn, potatoes, and cucumbers and wondered how that must be affecting stream flow in Settlers Creek.

C.J. was just about to call Maggie, to find out how the protest march in Minneapolis had gone, when his phone rang.

"Hi, C.J.," a tired-sounding Maggie said.

"Hi back to you, Maggie," said C.J. "I was just about to call you."

"Thought you'd to like to hear how the march in Minneapolis went on Saturday."

"I'm all ears," said C.J. as he scratched Lucky's head.

"Well, to be brutally frank about it, not so good," said Maggie.

"How so?"

"To start with, only about a hundred people showed up. We were expecting a thousand. And we really hadn't planned the protest march well. The only idea we had was to march around the Minneapolis offices of the Al-Mid Pipeline Company."

"Sounds reasonable," said C.J.

"This will sound dumb, but we should have realized that the offices would be closed on a Saturday. And they were. So we marched around an empty building, albeit a big building, for a couple hours. We had no opportunity to talk with any of the pipeline officials."

"Didn't people talk with you and find out what you were protesting?" asked C.J.

"Several people did ask what we were doing. I talked to one woman who said we should have stayed home and minded our own business. Talked to another fellow who said he never heard of Link Lake or any disabled veterans farming in Settlers Valley. He also said he supports pipelines because they are a lot safer than hauling oil on trains. We did get the thumbs-up from several others. But I don't think many people understood what we were protesting," said Maggie.

"Did the Twin Cities newspapers cover the march?" asked C.J.

"Sort of," said Maggie. "I saw a brief paragraph in the back pages of the local news in the Sunday *Minneapolis Sun*. I'll read it to you. The headline was 'Another Protest March.' 'A scant hundred protestors carrying signs that read "Stop the Pipeline" marched in front of the U.S. headquarters for the Al-Mid Pipeline Company on Hennepin Avenue Saturday. The group was protesting the pipeline company's plan to build in Settlers Valley in Ames County, Wisconsin. They apparently did not have an opportunity to meet with any officials of the pipeline company, which one protestor said had been their goal.'"

"That's it for the newspaper coverage? Any TV stories, radio interviews?" asked C.J.

"Nope. Nothing. The media apparently thought our group was too small to give us any attention. An older person I talked with who seemed sympathetic to what we were trying to do said, 'Maybe you should protest closer to home.' I think he has a point, based on what I saw and heard on Saturday. Besides, it's expensive to protest in Minneapolis. Do you know that Pastor Vicki and I had to pay 250 dollars for a hotel room Saturday night? Vicki said the motel in Link Lake charges sixty dollars a night."

C.J. laughed at Maggie's last comment about the motel room. "From what you are saying, we'd better do some rethinking about how we'll keep this pipeline out of Settlers Valley."

"Yes, and we'd better get right at it. I haven't heard a word from the pipeline company. Have you?" asked Maggie.

"Nope, nothing. My guess is they're waiting for tempers to cool a bit in Settlers Valley before they make their next move."

"Something else I discovered," said Maggie, changing the subject.

"What would that be?"

"Well, ever since I saw that engineer from the pipeline company prancing through my sweet corn patch and acting like he owned the place, I've been doing a little digging."

"Digging where?"

"Right here at home. I dug out the papers we signed when we received ownership of our farms from the Josh Barnes Memorial Homestead fund. Do you know that homestead contract is ten pages long? I don't think any of us read every page, we were just so darn happy to be getting our farms essentially for nothing," Maggie said.

"So? I'm afraid I've signed contracts like that. But in every case I made sure I trusted the person I was contracting with," said C.J.

"What I'm going to do," said Maggie, "is send a copy of my homestead contract to my lawyer friend at the Pentagon. But I must say, I wanted to trust the Herman Barnes Family Foundation. I can image the grief Mr. Barnes experienced when he lost his son in the war. And I can understand his wanting to help a bunch of disabled veterans in the name of his son. I feel a little guilty about having my friend take a closer look. Don't tell anybody. I sure don't want the Herman Barnes Family Foundation to think I'm checking up on my homestead grant behind their back."

"Mum's the word," said C.J.

# 42

For the next several days, C.J. worked in his garden, hoeing and watering. Watering and hoeing. It had become a ritual. Every night he looked to the west to see if he could spot any rain clouds. But there were none. If the day had been a windy one, the sun set in a dirty-yellow sky, sending eerie, ominous light over the landscape. It was as if someone had put a yellow-brown filter over the sun. Ever since he had spent summers at his grandpa Oscar's, evening on the farm had been C.J.'s favorite time. In the evening, during the warm months, C.J. and Lucky sat on the porch looking out over Settlers Valley and the little stream that threaded through it. During these dry days, the small stream was not as deep and flowed less rapidly than when rainfall in the valley was ample. But it continued to flow. C.J. had heard that one of the streams near Stevens Point had ceased flowing one summer because there was too much irrigation going on in the area.

C.J. continued to deliver fresh vegetables to the grocery cooperative twice a week. He tried to keep up a regular routine, which meant he also spent some time nearly every day writing in his journal. When he first began journaling at the suggestion of one of the doctors at Walter Reed, he discovered that writing helped him make sense out of what was happening in his life.

Now he wrote:

Wednesday, July 31

Another sunny day. Not a cloud in the sky as the several-weeks-long drought continues. Today, I'm thinking about all that has happened in Link Lake and Settlers Valley over the past few months. Most recently, who killed Ben Rostom's chickens and stole a couple of them besides? Only a sick-minded person would slit the throats of those beautiful market-ready broilers, leaving them to die in a pile of torn feathers on a blood-soaked chicken house floor. If he only wanted to steal a couple of chickens, why did he have to kill a bunch more? It makes no sense.

So much of what has been happening this year in Link Lake and Settlers Valley makes no sense. Who would burn down a church? That's about as sick a deed as anything I have ever heard of. Who would shoot at a U.S. senator trying to help disabled veterans with his legislative activity? I can't believe a segment of the U.S. population is so down on us disabled vets that they would do this. Maybe it's several people. I wish Maggie and the sheriff would get this figured out. These are tough times in Settlers Valley, especially with the drought hanging on day after day, week after week. To add to the misery, the damn pipeline company seems hell-bent on running roughshod across our farms. That is the last thing we need.

Increasingly, C.J. felt the old feelings of guilt, like the feelings he had when he left the service with one leg missing, but at least he was still alive. Several of his fellow soldiers hadn't made it. For a while, thanks to his work here in Settlers Valley, he had begun to feel better. But now once more he felt the dreaded pangs of guilt that came to him in the night, keeping him from sleeping. It had been his idea to invite some of his fellow wounded vets to Settlers Valley. And now everything seemed to be falling apart. He felt helpless, unsure which way to turn, what to do, or what to say to his fellow veterans. He had thought he was leading them to a place where he and they could recover from their wounds, but recent circumstances had only added to their misery. He opened the cupboard door and stared at his old friend Jack Daniels. Was the answer to his personal misery in this bottle?

C.J. was jolted out of his dark thoughts by the ringing of his cell phone.

"This is C.J.," he said. He hoped his voice didn't sound as hopeless as he felt.

"It's Maggie. Can I stop over?"

"Sure, what's up?"

"I'll be there in a few minutes."

*Now what?* thought C.J. *Maggie upset with me just when we've patched things up?*

Maggie parked her ancient Toyota next to C.J.'s pickup. She was carrying a stack of papers.

"Have a seat," said C.J. He pointed to the empty rocking chair sitting next to him. "What's going on?"

"Remember me saying I was sending a copy of my homestead contract to my lawyer friend at the Pentagon?"

"Did you hear from her?"

"I did. And guess what? Stuck in the midst of some fine print that recited the history of the 1862 Homestead Act, she found a secondary list of stipulations that referred to the money we've gotten from the Herman Barnes Family Foundation. On the first page of the contract, in large print, the contract states that if we agreed to the provisions of the contract, we would gain ownership of our land in five years. All we had to do was live on the property, till the land, and show improvements each year."

"Right," said C.J.

"Well, after reading the contract a couple of times, she found, stuck in the middle of page 8, this language: 'Recipients of this homestead grant, within the five years of their probationary time, must allow any person or persons working for the public interest to have access to this land.'"

"On first reading, she thought the words sounded innocuous. Sort of a feel-good, throwaway line. I told my friend about the fellow traipsing across my land. My friend said that one line in the contract gave permission to the pipeline company to build on my land. It would also give permission to an electric transmission power company, telephone company, or any business or organization doing 'work for the public interest,'" said Maggie.

"In other words, the disabled vets with homestead contracts have signed away their rights?" asked C.J.

"It appears so," said a dejected-sounding Maggie.

"And it makes no sense for you vets to protest something that's a done deal in the eyes of the law?" asked C.J., now feeling even more miserable than he did before Maggie arrived.

"Yup," said Maggie. "But the rest of you, and Oscar and Fred can still protest, and I for one will help. The school forest people surely don't want a pipeline running across their property. All of you can protest. My friend also checked some other court cases and discovered that the courts did proclaim pipelines as being in the public interest."

"Jeez," is all C.J. could think to say.

The two sat quietly, not saying anything for a few minutes.

Maggie broke the silence. "By the way, C.J., when's it going to rain?"

"I wish I knew . . . I wish I knew," said C.J. with a sigh.

# 43

After Maggie left, C.J. was both confused and angry. Could it be true that the homestead contract's seemingly boilerplate language gave permission to companies like the Al-Mid Pipeline Company to build on the disabled veterans' farms without any further consent? Maggie, a former military police detective, believed it was so.

For a few minutes, C.J. sat on his porch, Lucky's head on his knee. The dog looked up at him as if he knew the anguish that C.J. was feeling, the confusion that was threading through his mind.

*How will the other vets react when they learn that they have to allow the pipeline company to build on their land?* thought C.J.

He had an idea. He picked up his cell phone and made a call.

"This is Pastor Vicki," C.J. heard after the phone had rung a couple of times.

"Vicki, this is C.J. Do you have some time to talk? Can we meet at the Eat Well at one thirty this afternoon?"

"Sure, that'll work for me. What's going on?"

"I'm afraid I have some more bad news," said C.J., sounding a bit defeated.

Most of the noon-hour business had departed when C.J. arrived at the restaurant and found Pastor Vicki sitting at one of the tables in the back, nursing a cup of coffee.

"Thanks for meeting at such short notice," said C.J.

"Happy to do it. Want some coffee?"

C.J. turned to see the waitress standing behind him with an empty cup and a coffee pot.

"Sure," said C.J.

Turning to Pastor Vicki, C.J. said, "How's the building coming?"

"Faster than I thought. The builders have about completed my little apartment that will be in the back of the church. The contractor told me that by October 1, we should be able to hold church services there once more. Good news!" said Pastor Vicki, smiling.

"Well, I'm afraid I have more bad news," said C.J.

"Story of my life," said Pastor Vicki. "Good news and bad news seem to come in pairs. So what's the bad news?"

C.J. explained how Maggie had sent her homestead contract to a lawyer friend at the Pentagon.

"What did she learn?"

"There's a line in the contract that on the surface appears innocuous but likely isn't." C.J. dug into his pocket and pulled out a sheet of paper. "Here's what the line says: 'Recipients of this homestead grant, within the five years of their probationary time, must allow any person or persons working for the public interest to have access to this land.'

"Maggie's lawyer friend said that a pipeline company can be considered 'a public interest.' She looked at the records for an old court case involving the Al-Mid Pipeline Company and a northern Wisconsin farmer, one Jonas Symborski, who did not want the pipeline to cross his property. Al-Mid sued Symborski after he refused to lease his land to Al-Mid. Symborski argued that the construction of the pipeline was not a public use. Thus, he could not be forced to lease his land to Al-Mid. However, the Wisconsin Supreme Court ruled that 'the location of pipelines for transmitting, transporting, storing, or delivering natural gas or oil is in the public interest' and Mr. Symborski lost the case. I think the disabled vets who signed those homestead contracts are screwed, if you'll pardon my language."

"C.J., this is serious stuff. What do we do?" asked Pastor Vicki.

"Well, if I know Maggie, and I think I know her pretty well, she's not gonna rest until she gets to the bottom of this tangled mess," said C.J.

"That homestead money all flowed through our church," said Pastor Vicki, her alarm growing. "We should have had a lawyer check those contracts before encouraging the vets to sign them. Maybe we could have headed all of this off."

"The problem is we all saw this homestead money hanging out there for the picking, with few strings attached. We trusted Richard Barnes with his story about how his son died in Iraq and we applauded the Herman Barnes Family Foundation for what they wanted to do for the disabled vets here in Settlers Valley. Some days I wish I had never started this project. All it seems to be doing is bringing trouble to this community," said C.J.

"Hey," said Pastor Vicki as she put her hand on C.J.'s arm. "Quit kicking yourself. It's not your fault that all of this is happening. We'll work this through. We really will."

"I'm not so sure," said C.J. "Everything, and I mean everything, looks mighty bleak these days. Even the weather is against us."

"C.J., quit it. There's always hope. Keep hoping. That's what farmers do a lot of, I'm told," said Pastor Vicki, smiling.

# 44

C.J. had just finished breakfast. He sat in his favorite rocking chair on the cabin porch, rocking and watching the mists rise from the valley. He and Lucky watched a pair of sandhill cranes, with two little ones, walking along the creek bank, searching for something to eat. *What a beautiful bird*, thought C.J.

"Another dry day," he said. Lucky looked at his master as if understanding the words. "When is it gonna rain?"

The drought had become severe. For more than a week, there had been little wind, lots of sunshine, and near ninety-degree temperatures. With some moisture, all of the crops would be flourishing. *Every living thing needs sunlight, but every living thing also needs water,* C.J. thought.

He was deep in his thoughts when his cell phone rang.

"It's Maggie," the familiar voice said.

"Good morning," said C.J.

"Just had a call from the sheriff," Maggie said. "Got a problem in the school forest. Somebody is lost in the woods."

"A kid?"

"No, it's one of the pipeline engineers who was apparently doing a little unofficial looking around and got himself lost," said Maggie.

"Didn't the guy have his phone with him?"

"C.J., it all sounds a little strange. This engineer and the lease guy, Emory Sage, are staying in a motel in Willow River. Sage said the engineer didn't return to the motel last night. He didn't call, so Sage figured he must have lost his cell phone or there was no connection. Anyway, the sheriff is putting together a posse to look for the guy. I'm contacting all the vets to see if they can help look for him. We're to meet at the school forest shelter building at nine this morning," said Maggie.

"I'll be there," said C.J.

When C.J. arrived at the school forest, the parking lot was already nearly full. He spotted Maggie talking with the sheriff and joined them.

"Listen up," the sheriff said into a bullhorn. "We've got a guy lost in these woods, and he may be injured. His name is Bud Jenkins. Here's the plan. I want us to form a line and walk slowly through the woods. I'll call his name every so often with the bullhorn, and we'll listen for a response."

The line quickly formed and slowly began moving through the woods, with the sheriff calling, "Bud, Bud Jenkins," every few minutes. Everyone strained to hear a response to the sheriff's calls, but there was no sound. It was dead quiet in the woods. There was no wind, and with the drought, all the wild animals and birds seemed to have hunkered down near a water source.

As C.J. walked along, looking behind a fallen tree, searching a thicket of blackberry bushes, looking left, looking right, he was thinking about the irony of the situation. It was no secret that the disabled veterans despised the idea of a pipeline crossing their farms, yet here they were searching for a pipeline engineer who was apparently lost in the woods and maybe hurt.

"Bud, Bud Jenkins, this is Sheriff Jansen. Can you hear me?" The sound of Jansen's voice once more broke the silence of the morning and reminded C.J. to pay attention to the task.

The group was only a few hundred yards into the woods when C.J. heard Maggie's voice. "Over here," she yelled. "I've found him. Over here."

C.J., closest to where Maggie was walking, yelled, "Where are you?"

"I'm at the creek bank, west of the shelter house," Maggie yelled back.

C.J. hurried toward Maggie and soon saw her bending over something. At a distance, he couldn't see what it was.

"I think I've found Mr. Jenkins," Maggie said when C.J. got closer. "He's been shot."

"Is he . . . is he dead?" C.J. said, viewing the body sprawled face-down in the forest duff.

"Yes, he's dead," Maggie said. "Shot with a high-powered rifle, from the size of the wound."

"What next?" said C.J. "Who in the world did this?"

Maggie used her sheriff's department radio to call it in since there was no cell phone connection in the thick woods. "Sheriff'll be right along," she said. "He'll call the coroner. And he reminded us not to touch anything." Maggie rolled her eyes. "Sometimes I think he forgets I was an MP detective."

While they waited for the sheriff, she and C.J. heard another person yelling.

"Over here," yelled a voice that Maggie and C.J. could barely make out. "I've found a body."

"What the hell?" said C.J. "What is going on?"

"I wish I knew," said Maggie, once more on the radio to the sheriff. "Well, Mr. Jenkins isn't going anywhere. Let's see what this is all about." A deputy had now arrived. Maggie said, "Could you stay with this body?"

"Where are you?" yelled C.J., cupping his hands around his mouth.

"I'm north of you," C.J. heard in response.

"Yell every couple minutes," C.J. said.

"Okay," C.J. heard faintly.

C.J. and Maggie hurried in the direction of the yells, into a section of the woods where there were no trails and the area was thick with brush and downed trees. Walking was difficult, and while the dry weather had eliminated the mosquitoes in most open areas, not so here in these deep woods among the black oak, white oak, and the occasional white birch trees. There was no hint of a breeze as C.J. and Maggie plodded on, swatting mosquitoes and swabbing the sweat from their eyes. The last yell they heard was much closer. Through the thick forest undercover, they caught a glimpse of a man waving, as he had apparently spotted C.J. and Maggie before they saw him.

"Over here," a deputy sheriff yelled. He'd earlier discovered the battery on his radio was dead.

Stumbling into a small clearing, they saw that a huge tree had blown down, its root mass standing at least four feet high. "I'm Deputy Calendar," the young man said. He was tall and thin and deeply tanned.

"C.J. Anderson and Maggie Werth," Maggie said, extending her hand.

"I know you," Deputy Calendar said as he looked more closely at Maggie. "You've been working with our department as a consultant. A former military police detective, right?"

"Yes," said Maggie. "What have you got here?"

"Well, what's here is pretty awful, can't say I've seen anything quite like it," the deputy said.

"Looks like a wilderness camp," said C.J., glancing at the camouflaged tent nearly hidden behind the fallen tree roots.

"Not easily seen," said the deputy. "I stumbled onto it . . . almost walked by without even seeing it. Look in the tent."

C.J. pulled back the tent flap, and he and Maggie glanced into the dim interior of the tent.

"Oh my God," said Maggie, holding her hand to her mouth.

"Wow," said C.J. "What happened?" he said, looking at the deputy who stood nearby, looking like he might throw up.

"Looks to me like this guy was hiding out here in the woods and decided to shoot himself in the head. He still has the pistol in his hand," said the deputy.

"Who is he?" asked C.J., who saw that the upper part of the man's head was blown away.

"I didn't touch anything, so I don't know," said the deputy.

In a few minutes, Sheriff Jansen arrived on the scene, sweating and swatting mosquitoes.

"Whatta ya got here?"

"Another dead guy. This one looks like a suicide," said the deputy.

"We haven't had a murder or a suicide in Ames County for ten years. Good God, now we got two dead guys in one day. What the hell is going on?" said the sheriff.

The sheriff lifted the tent flap and looked in. "What a mess. Well, let's drag what's left of this guy out of this damn tent and see if he's got any ID on him. You guys give me a hand." He pointed to C.J. and the deputy.

Slowly they dragged the corpse out into the open and the sheriff looked for the man's wallet, which he found in his back pocket. "Driver's license says the guy's name is Randy Budwell. Any of you know a Randy Budwell?"

"Oh, no. I do," said C.J. "He was one of the original group of disabled vets who came here to farm. I met him when we were together back at Walter Reed about three years ago."

"How in the world did he end up in this scruffy little tent hidden away here in the woods?" asked the sheriff.

"Boy, I sure don't know," said C.J. rubbing his hand through his black beard. "He never took to farming, never liked it, and never learned how to do it. And he had a drinking problem. Last I heard he was in the veterans hospital in Madison. He had a bad case of PTSD.

I really thought working a small farm would help him. It obviously didn't."

"Wonder what pushed him over the edge?" said Maggie. "Something surely triggered this."

"We'll probably never know," said the sheriff. "Deputy Calendar, would you stay here until the coroner comes, then could you clean up this mess, take down the tent, and gather up any personal belongings you can find?"

"Sure," the deputy said.

# 45

"Looks like little Link Lake and our peaceful Settlers Valley has gotten just like a big city," said Fred as he sat across from Oscar at the Eat Well.

"How do you figure that?" asked Oscar.

"Read about it in the paper. I'm sure you also heard about it from C.J. We got ourselves a murder and a suicide on the same day."

"This ain't us," said Oscar. "I don't know what in the hell is going on. But murders and suicides just don't happen here."

"But they did, Oscar," said Fred. "They happened right here in the school forest of all places. You read about the disabled vet who'd been living in a little tent deep in the forest?"

"I did," said Oscar. "I also read that the search party for the lost engineer guy stumbled onto a black pickup that was covered with a camouflaged tarp, with brush piled on top of it. The story said one of the searchers almost walked right into it before he saw it was a hidden truck. Sheriff figured the truck belonged to the vet that committed suicide. Beyond hiding his camp and his truck, the guy had cleverly covered up the truck's tracks. He'd found an old logging road that led from where he hid his truck out to the county road."

"Did you know this vet?" asked Fred.

"Not really. I remember plowing maybe five acres for him shortly after he came here to Settlers Valley and rented what he called his lost acres. I remember him asking, 'What am I doing here? In the middle of nowhere. Trying to be a farmer. I am no farmer.' I remember him saying that, and thinking it was a little strange that he had agreed to come here feeling the way he did," said Oscar. "But I also thought that maybe doing a little digging in the dirt could help the guy. He sounded so negative."

"I guess we can't win them all," said Fred. "But what in the world would possess the guy to commit suicide? I guess we may never know. Heard anything from the sheriff as to who killed the pipeline engineer who was snooping around in the school forest?"

"I haven't. Not a word from the sheriff," said Oscar.

"Suppose there is some connection between the two?" asked Fred.

"Sheriff is looking into that theory, but so far he doesn't see any connection, even though they happened on the same day."

"It's a damned, horrible mess. That's what it is," said Fred. "One damn thing after another. And now one of the worst droughts this area has experienced in ten years," said Fred. "What are these vets going to go on? How're they gonna make it?"

# 46

The dry weather continued, but Settlers Creek continued flowing, providing for a green strip of grass on either side before the green turned to brown, as the wild plants waited for rain, along with all other life in the valley.

As he sat on his back porch on another hot and sunny morning, C.J.'s head was filled with thoughts about Randy Budwell's suicide. Why had he done it? He remembered meeting Randy at Walter Reed almost three years ago. Randy had lost one of his feet when the Humvee he was driving ran over an IED. One of his best friends was killed, and Randy had never gotten over believing that he was to blame. He told C.J. that had he been more alert, he would have spotted the IED. His commanding officer had said that no vehicles had encountered an IED on this particular road. So he wasn't watching the roadway as carefully as he had been trained to do.

C.J. had encouraged Randy to come with him to Settlers Valley. He shouldn't have. Randy had grown up in New York City. His parents had told him that whatever he did with his life, he should avoid the Midwest, where the people ate a strange sausage they call bratwurst, listened to polka music played on an accordion, drank lots of beer, and spent their winters fishing through the ice. His parents, professors of literature at Columbia University, had instructed their only son to avoid farming, which they considered the lowest of the low types of work. In addition to PTSD, Randy had a head full of "what not to do" ingrained in him by his parents.

C.J. heard these prejudices from Randy, but he was convinced that working the land and living in a rural community would change his thinking and it would also help Randy psychologically. *How wrong I was*, thought C.J. *I'm as sure as sure can be that I had something to do with Randy committing suicide.*

C.J. pounded his hand on the arm of the rocking chair, nearly spilling the half cup of coffee that sat on a little table nearby. "Dammit," C.J. said aloud. "Dammit to hell. Why do things like this keep happening to me? Why? Why? Why?" Lucky looked up at his master and whined as if the big dog felt some of his master's misery.

C.J. fished for his ringing cell phone that he carried in the front pocket of his jeans.

"Hello," he said, trying not to sound as depressed as he felt.

"This is Maggie. How're you doing today?" she asked.

"Not well, Maggie, not well. I can't get Randy Budwell's suicide out of my mind. It's my fault, you know."

"Quit beating up on yourself, C.J. You and I both know that when someone is that far gone, no one person could have stopped them," Maggie said.

"I'd like to believe you, Maggie. I really would. But it's hard," C.J. said.

"I've got some good news from a bad situation, which I think you will find most interesting," Maggie said, trying to sound cheerful. "Will you help me call the Back to the Land Veterans and invite them to attend a special meeting? I've talked to your grandpa, and he gave us permission to meet in his barn."

"Sure, I'll make some calls for you," said C.J.

That afternoon the entire group of disabled veterans gathered in Oscar Anderson's hay loft. All the farmers were there as well as Pastor Vicki and Tommy Green, who managed the grocery cooperative.

It was a hot August afternoon, but with fans going, it was reasonably comfortable in the old barn.

"Thank you all for coming," said Maggie. "You'll notice that I also invited Sheriff Jansen to this meeting. Thanks for coming, Floyd," Maggie said. She turned to the sheriff, who stood up and began speaking.

"I'm pleased to see all of you here this afternoon," said the sheriff. "I know it was short notice, but I believe we have some good news to share with you. I wish we could say that rain is on its way, but I believe you will find what we have discovered to be most interesting. Much of what we have learned is due to Maggie's sharp eye and careful attention to detail. You are fortunate in having a fellow farmer with excellent investigation skills. I'll let Maggie tell you what we've just learned."

Maggie stood up again and began. "We were all saddened to learn about our fellow veteran, Randy Budwell. I know several of you knew him, and I know that you, Pastor Vicki, knew him quite well. It was Deputy Jules Calendar who stumbled onto Randy's camp in Link Lake's school forest while many of us were looking for the lost pipeline engineer. As you all know, the engineer was shot and killed.

"After finding Randy's body, Sheriff Jansen asked Deputy Calendar to take down the tent and clean up the campsite. He found the trail camera, with Randy's picture on it, carrying vegetables he filched from the school garden. Deputy Calendar found Randy's sniper rifle carefully hidden under the side of the tent. Now we know that he had two sniper rifles, the one he used when he shot at Senator Shelburne, and this one. Almost by accident, I found a letter when I was looking through the stuff Deputy Calendar had removed from the tent. Here's a copy." Maggie held up several pages of paper. She smoothed out the wrinkled paper on the little podium that stood in front of her and began reading.

To my fellow veterans,

It is with a heavy heart that I write these words. When you read them, I will be dead. Taking my life has become my only choice as I have made many bad decisions during the past several months. I shot the man that I know you must have found. I did not plan to kill him but merely wanted to scare him away as I feared he might find my camp where I have lived the past several months. I know most of you think I am in the hospital in Madison. And I was. But I escaped the clutches of the head doctors who were supposed to help me and didn't. I returned to Settlers Valley, which is a pretty good place to live.

I was angry. Mad at the military that put me in harm's way. Mad at my commanding officer, who said the road we were traveling in Afghanistan was safe for travel. Mad at myself for allowing my best friend to be killed. I brought my anger with me when I returned to Link Lake and Settlers Valley. Envy also overtook me when I returned and saw you, my fellow veterans, working your little farms, gathering at Pastor Vicki's church. I burned the church. I didn't plan for it to burn to the ground. I only wanted to start a little fire so that Pastor Vicki would leave and abandon what she was doing.

Pastor Vicki, I was so wrong. You are a good person. You tried to help me. But I refused your help and wanted to help myself by making friends with a whiskey bottle. It was I who disrupted the church services in Oscar Anderson's barn. I shot Oscar's dog. I didn't mean to do that either. I only wanted it to stop barking. I know it now, but madness can sometimes turn to meanness. I disrupted the rhubarb festival and messed up your little grocery. Why? I was tired of seeing how well you all were doing. And the shot that missed the senator: I could have killed him. Probably should have since all the senator's words about how disabled veterans are not adequately cared for are mostly words with little action. The government is still not taking care of us. And yes, I tried to scare the kids at the school forest when they were there on an overnight. I just didn't want one of them to go stumbling through the woods and spot my camp. I stole vegetables from the school forest garden. I did have to eat. And I killed Ben Rostom's chickens. I only wanted to take two of them, but killing the others was so easy.

Lastly, I want to thank C.J. Anderson. I met C.J. at Walter Reed Hospital; he was suffering as I was. C.J.is a great guy. I only wish I hadn't let him down. I really wasn't cut out to be a farmer. That's just the truth. Why couldn't I be like the rest of you disabled veterans who seem to be healing? I now know that working the land can heal, but not everyone can benefit. I thought I would make it. I was wrong.

I close with these words: There is a time for living, and there is a time for dying. This is my dying time.

Your fellow veteran, Randy Budwell

Maggie folded the papers and stepped away from the podium. The only sound in the vast open space of the old barn was an English sparrow chattering away as it sat on one of the barn's massive wooden beams.

# 47

C.J. returned home that afternoon both saddened and relieved. He was mourning the loss of a friend who had sunk to the pits of despair and could only see suicide as the answer to his sick mind. He was relieved to learn that the mystery of who had been causing all the disruption in Settlers Valley over the past several months had been solved. But two things still worried him. The valley desperately needed rain. And what about the dreaded pipeline about to plow right across Settlers Valley, disrupting the struggling disabled vets who were trying to make a living on their small-acreage farms?

As C.J. hoed in his garden, his thoughts were all about his fellow disabled veterans and the possibility that they had no recourse but to allow the pipeline to build on their properties. *What a mess*, he thought. With all the turmoil in Settlers Valley, C.J. hadn't felt well. He hadn't been sleeping. He hadn't been eating well. He had been worrying nonstop about his fellow disabled vets. Now he wondered if he was coming down with something. Maybe the flu. His leg with the prosthesis had been serving him well. But today it hurt, especially where the prosthesis was attached just below his knee. What was going on with that?

Cutting off weeds with his hoe, C.J. noticed that he was sweating more than he usually did. He had glanced at the thermometer before coming out into the garden. It read eighty degrees. The temperature had been hanging around eighty degrees for the last few weeks, so why did he feel warmer today? Lucky, who usually walked alongside him as he worked in the garden, was sprawled out under a shade tree. C.J. thought, *That dog is smarter than I am. Why am I out here soaked in sweat when I could be sitting under a tree, in the shade?*

C.J. realized that for the first time in a month, the humidity had come up. That's why he was sweating. *Duh,* he thought. During the summers that he worked on his grandfather's farm, Oscar had tried to show him the basics of weather predicting. One of them was the humidity. When the humidity rose, it usually meant that rain was on the way. *Could that be the case now? Is rain finally coming?* C.J. thought as he took off his hat and wiped the perspiration from his sweating forehead. *A soaking rain would surely help our struggling crops.*

That evening it was stiflingly hot in C.J.'s cabin. All the windows were open, but there was no wind, not even a hint of an evening breeze. C.J. recalled Grandpa Oscar calling a hot summer evening like this one "close."

C.J. and Lucky sat on the porch after C.J. had finished supper and washed his dishes. As he sat in the rocking chair, gently rocking, C.J. noticed how quiet it was. Nothing was stirring. Off in the distance, he heard an owl calling, "Who cooks for you? Who cooks for you?" And from another direction, an owl returned the call. C.J.'s imagination kicked in. He wondered what these owls were talking about, wondered if they were discussing a place where they might meet on this muggy, summer evening.

And then, only a few yards away in the direction of Settlers Creek, he heard a whip-poor-will call its name over and over. He counted ten times. And then it was quiet once more, eerily quiet as the sun slipped away to the west, with both Lucky and C.J. watching. C.J. was wondering if it was his imagination, or did he see a bank of clouds, just easing above the horizon? Or was it merely wishful thinking?

By nine thirty, with darkness having engulfed the valley once more, C.J. removed his prosthesis and crawled into bed. Lucky had his run of the place, and on this hot and humid night, the big dog chose to remain on the porch. C.J. wondered if this would be another night of nightmares and no sleep, as had been the case for at least half of the nights in the past two weeks. Working hard in the garden every day made him physically tired, but how he wished his mind so cluttered with memories and worries could be turned off.

Something woke C.J. At first he thought it might have been the wind, for he felt a cool breeze filtering through his bedroom window. But then he heard it. Thunder. A rolling, growling thunder. Glancing out the window, he saw a jagged slice of lightning cut through a bank of angry black clouds. Lucky was scratching on the kitchen door, wanting in from the porch. The big dog hadn't been in the house more than a minute when the first big drops of rain, flying on a wind that became ever stronger, began striking the kitchen window that he had just closed. The raindrops skidded down the windowpane to the windowsill. C.J. hoped that this storm was not one of those quickie ones that boiled up out of the west, made a lot of noise, and then moved east, leaving behind but a few drops of rain.

C.J. and Lucky watched the storm from the kitchen window as the black clouds rolled up Settlers Valley and the lightning zigged and zagged across the black sky. He heard the wind tear around the corners of his sturdy log cabin, rattling the windows. C.J. smiled because it was raining. Raining hard. Pouring down rain. Raining cats and dogs, as Grandpa Oscar would say.

C.J. went to back to bed with a smile on his face. He listened to the rain pound against his bedroom window. A wonderful sound. A sound of hope. He was soon fast asleep, sleeping more deeply than he had in weeks.

He awakened with Lucky licking his face, reminding him that it was morning, although it was still quite dark. He got up, put on his prosthetic leg, and hobbled out to the kitchen with Lucky at his side. He let the big dog outside and immediately saw that the rain had not let up, that the rain clouds had not moved east but looked thick and rich with water.

C.J. pulled on his rain jacket and cap and walked out to look at his rain gauge, which for the past several weeks had collected dust but now was nearly running over with water. C.J. looked a second time. It showed six inches of rain. Could it have rained that much overnight? C.J. looked out over the valley, which he could only dimly see. When he had stepped outside, he heard a roaring sound that he couldn't quite identify. Now, through the mist and the pouring rain, he saw a Settlers Creek the likes of which he had not seen before. The creek was three times its average size, flooding the ground around it and roaring on its way to the Fox River and on to Lake Winnebago.

Would Settlers Valley move from drought to flood? It crossed C.J.'s mind as he put out Lucky's food bowl and filled it with dog food before he prepared his own breakfast. As he watched the roaring creek, he was glad he had listened to his grandfather, who had said, no matter how beautiful it might be to have your home close to a river, don't build there. Always build on high ground. *I'm glad I took Grandpa's advice*, thought C.J.

# 48

As Oscar and Fred sat at their regular table in the Eat Well, rain pounded against the nearby window. Both old men sat watching the rain, not saying a word, enjoying what they were seeing.

"Well, Oscar, it's happenin'," said Fred.

"Yup, it sure is," said Oscar, smiling. "Took a while, but it's sure comin' down. Checked my rain gauge this morning and it read six inches—and it's still comin'. Boy, we sure needed it."

"City people don't talk much about rain. At least not like we farmers do. Farmers know that a good rain can make the difference between a decent crop and no crop at all," said Fred.

"I remember so well those droughty years of the 1930s," said Oscar. "We grew about twenty acres of alfalfa and clover mix for hay. I think it was either 1937 or 1938 when we got but two wagonloads of hay from that twenty acres. That's all there was. It wasn't much good either. Mostly stems. I remember Pa turned to cut marsh hay that grew along Settlers Creek bottomland. Marsh hay doesn't have a whole lot of power in it, but it got us through the long, cold winter. The same thing happened with the corn. Pa always grew about twenty acres of corn. Planted it in May with a two-row horse-pulled planter. We had a little rain in the spring that year, but by the end of June, just like this year, no rain. The corn grew to about five feet tall, and it just stood there. Stopped growing. By August, it had begun to dry up, to turn brown, with ears about half the size they should be. Pa put the whole field of corn in the silo, and it still only filled the silo about two-thirds. Tough times. But you know, Fred, farmers, no matter how tough the year, how little it rained—or some years, when it rained too much—farmers always had hope. Hope that the next year would be better."

"Yup, Oscar, you are sure right about that. If we farmers didn't have hope, some years we'd have nothin'. Hope. It's a powerful thing. That's for sure," said Fred.

"Talkin' about hope," Oscar began, "I can't believe what this Randy Budwell did. That kid was sick. His mind wasn't right, or he wouldn't have done all those terrible things. Imagine killin' that pipeline engineer. And then killin' himself. I tell you, Fred, it's those damn wars that did it. When we gonna put a stop to these wars? What do they accomplish? Tell me that? What good comes out of these damn wars? A few rich guys get to line their pockets with more money, and some power-hungry bastard gets a little more power."

"How right you are, Oscar. Just look who suffers because of these wars. You don't have to look beyond Settlers Valley. Every one of these young Back to the Land Veterans has suffered. Often in more ways than we could ever imagine. That's to say nothin' about the thousands of other people, mostly ordinary folks tryin' to make a livin' and raise a family. They suffer. They suffer terribly. When's it gonna stop?" asked Fred. "When in hell are we gonna stop these damn wars?"

"I wish I knew," said Oscar. "I sure wish I knew."

Oscar and Fred both sat quietly for a time, looking out the window. Watching the falling rain.

"Back to that poor bugger Randy Budwell. His personal sufferin' turned into sufferin' for lots of folks. Part of me feels sorry for the guy, especially when the world looked hopeless to him." Oscar bit into the huge sweet roll that he had ordered. Then he continued. "Another part of me wants to kick Budwell's ass. I was hopin' by now—and C.J. would probably hate me for sayin' it—but I was hopin' the newspapers and the TV people would want to do stories about how these disabled vets were showin' the way for a new kind of farmin'. Farmin' that follows the motto that my dad often said: 'When you take care of the land, it will take care of you.' These disabled vets are takin' that one step further. 'As you help heal the land, it will in turn help heal you.'" Oscar paused and took another bite of his sweet roll.

"What happened?" he went on. "All the attention has been on the wild spree of destruction that Budwell brought to the valley. All the news has been negative, leading the TV watchers and the newspaper readers to believe that Settlers Valley is the worst place in the country to live. They should be talkin' about the successes of these Settlers Valley vets and how they are making a livin' on small-acreage farms. How they have rediscovered what community means by helpin' one another, by organizin' their own grocery cooperative, by showin' people livin' in this area how good fresh vegetables and fruits really are. How they are improvin' the land as they make a livin' on it. All of that has been lost in the fog of destruction and disruption that Budwell and his sickness brought to Link Lake and Settlers Valley. These disabled vets, bless them, keep on workin', keep on hopin' for better days. Of course, that damn pipeline is still plannin' to build, givin' everybody a headache, me included." He stopped to take a long drink of coffee.

"At least it's rainin'," said Fred, once more glancing out the window.

# 49

Not able to work in his garden on this rainy morning, C.J. sat at his kitchen table. He remembered telling the doctor who had suggested journaling that such writing was for teenage girls who wrote about their first loves. C.J. recalled what the doctor had said: "Journal writing is for everyone, young and old, rural, urban, military, or civilian. Journal writing is a way of keeping track of your life, its ups and downs, its joys and challenges. For those who need healing, journaling can help with that too."

C.J. remembered his doctor's words as he opened his journal, which had a well-worn leather cover, and began writing.

August 20
68 degrees at 7:00 a.m.
Raining
Thank you, God, for the rain. Thank you for once more giving us life-assuring water. At no cost. We are so conditioned to believe that everything has a price, but rainwater is free. Of course, we can't tell anyone or anything that it should rain on a particular day. We can pray for rain and most of us do when it is as dry as it has been for the past several weeks. But we must wait for the rain to fall. No global company controls the rain, offers it for sale, and delivers it in amounts requested. Mother Nature

deals with our weather on her terms, not on our terms. As much as it pains me to write this, given how the recent drought has challenged all the farmers in Ames County, I hope that Mother Nature will continue to be in charge, even though we may be unhappy with some of her choices and her timing. At least no person, company, or government can control the weather.

I can't remember when I slept as well as I did last night as I heard raindrops drumming on my bedroom window. A wonderfully soothing, hopeful sound. A sound asserting that life will go on, for everyone knows that without water, life is quickly extinguished.

C.J. paused in his writing when his cell phone rang.

"It's Maggie."

"Enjoying the rain, Maggie?" C.J. asked.

"Sheriff just called, and we've got a problem in the valley. The windstorm last night ripped the roof off John Wilson's barn, and Settlers Creek is flooding his entire farmstead. He needs help. I'm calling all the disabled vets," said Maggie.

"I'm on my way," said C.J. as he hung up, pulled on his boots, and reached for his rain hat and coat.

"Be back soon, Lucky," he said as he patted the big dog on the head and walked out into the driving rain, now coming down even harder than it was an hour earlier.

The country road that threaded through the valley and connected all the farms was rutted and even partially washed out in places. C.J. pushed the button in his pickup for four-wheel drive as he slowly made his way to the Wilson farm. Upon arriving, he saw a crew of men filling sandbags and stacking them around the Wilson home. He saw Holstein cows everywhere, wading in water up to their bellies and bellowing loudly. Several men were trying to drive them away from their roofless barn, trying to move them to higher ground where they would be safe. C.J. walked past several little hutches that had housed calves. The water had risen to nearly the top of these hutches, drowning all the calves.

C.J. joined the crew, now assisted by disabled vets who continued to arrive. Everywhere it was pandemonium. People yelling, cows bellowing, and the rain continuing to fall in torrents. A big Holstein cow that C.J. was trying to drive away from the barn almost ran over him as she insisted on returning to the doomed barn, which had no roof and was flooded with about four feet of water. Arriving at the barn, the big cow slipped and fell, and her head went underwater. She did not get up.

Slowly some order began to return to the scene. C.J. spotted Grandpa Oscar working with a crew on the high ground west of the barn to build a temporary fence for the surviving cows that had been driven to this location. He saw Maggie working with the crew that was making a sandbag wall around the Wilson home.

By noon, the rain had stopped and the sun had come out. But the waters of Settlers Creek continued to rise to levels that not even Oscar Anderson remembered. Much of the land in the valley looked like a lake, with no hint of where the creek once flowed quietly and gently. It appeared that the sandbagging crew had won a partial battle with the rising water and saved much of the Wilson home from significant flooding.

By now the electric company had arrived and turned off all the electricity. One of the linemen said he was surprised that the downed electrical wires hadn't killed anybody. Oscar and the crew had now successfully corralled the cattle; it was still unknown how many cows had died in the flood, but it would likely be a sizable number, in addition to the fifty or so calves that drowned. It would be several days before the water would recede enough to get a final count of how many animals succumbed.

There was little more the crew could do. C.J. chatted with several of his fellow veterans, inquiring about what damages they may have had from the flood. Outside of some washed-out vegetable patches, the vets had no significant losses. None of them lost any buildings or had any serious water damage.

As he was about to climb into his pickup, C.J. saw John Wilson signaling to him. Wilson's jacket was torn, he wore no cap or hat, and he had the look of someone who had been defeated.

"C.J.," Wilson said, his voice quivering. "Thank you so much. You didn't have to do this, you know."

"John, in spite of our differences, you are our neighbor. Neighbors help neighbors."

"So, how much do I owe you? How do I go about paying your whole group?" asked Wilson.

"John, you didn't hear me. You are our neighbor. When neighbors need help, we help. We'd expect the same from you. Nobody wants any of your money."

"Well, I just don't know what to say," said Wilson as he extended his hand to C.J.

"Nothing needs to be said. Are you and Florence going to be all right? All the power is off."

"I . . . I don't know," stammered Wilson.

"Tell you what. Until you get things back in order, why don't you and Florence come stay with me? I make my own power. And I'm all alone except for my dog, Lucky. I've got an extra bedroom."

"You would do that?" said Wilson.

"That's the least I can do. Besides, I don't think you and Florence want to take up residence at the motel in town. Good for a night or night or two, but . . . well, anyway, come on over at suppertime and plan to stay as long as you need to get things back in order."

"Oh, how can I ever thank you?" said Wilson, tears welling in his eyes. "You're probably wondering about the cows. I was just on my cell phone with the Lazy Z Dairy Farm. They're over in Winnebago County, and they said they have room for my cows. Good of them to offer. The first trucks should be here soon to haul my cows."

# 50

The Wilsons arrived at C.J.'s cabin a little after six. John Wilson carried a small suitcase that must have been in an upstairs closet since the basement and some of the first floor of their farm home had flooded. C.J. opened the kitchen door, with Lucky standing by his side, and beckoned them to come inside. The sun sat alone in a cloudless sky, a slight breeze blew from the southwest, and this fateful day was ending in stark contrast to when it had begun with pounding rain. C.J. noted that it had rained fifteen inches in the past two days, more rain than he had ever experienced in such a short period of time.

"Thank you so much for doin' this," said John Wilson as he and Florence stepped onto the porch. He looked like he had been run over by a truck. Wilson was in his late fifties, with a shock of graying hair that stuck out in every direction from his cap. His pants looked wet from sloshing around in the floodwater all day. Florence was only about five feet tall and thin as a fence post—that's how Oscar Anderson had described her. She looked like she had spent most of the day crying; her eyes were red and puffy, and her graying hair had not been combed.

Wilson patted Lucky's head. Immediately Wilson had another friend.

"I suspect you've got some dry clothes in that little suitcase," C.J. said. "I'll show you to the spare bedroom, where you can change and be more comfortable." Meanwhile, C.J. got busy preparing supper. When all else failed in the meal department, he turned to macaroni and cheese, which he now began to prepare on the old wood-burning cookstove. He also had some fresh lettuce and several ears of sweet corn, which he had harvested from his garden the day before the rains began. He placed the ears of corn in a pot of water that was soon boiling on the stove.

Wearing dry, clean clothes, the Wilsons walked into the kitchen.

"Supper's about ready," said C.J. "Find yourself a place at the table." Soon the three of them were enjoying macaroni and cheese, fresh garden lettuce, and—as Wilson described it—"about the best sweet corn I've ever eaten."

With supper finished, Florence Wilson said, "I'll do the dishes."

"No need," said C.J. "Just put them in the sink and come sit down."

But Florence began washing the dishes anyway, saying, "This is the least that we can do."

C.J. and John sat in the living room, in front of the window that looked out across Settlers Valley and Settlers Creek, still many times its normal size. With the window open, they could hear the roar of the rushing water.

"I'm so sorry for your loss," began C.J. "Never saw anything like it. Who would have thought that little Settlers Creek could go on such a rampage?"

"It was God's will," said John.

"How so?" asked C.J.

"God was telling me that expanding my dairy herd to a thousand cows was a bad idea, but I didn't listen," said John, holding his head in his hands. "I didn't listen. I didn't listen to my friend who operates the Lazy Z Farm, either. He advised me not to do it. He said milk prices aren't good and are likely not going to get much better. But I didn't listen. All I've been hearing is get bigger, or get out of business." He looked out the window at the flooded valley. "How'd your fellow vets survive the storm?" he asked, not wanting to think anymore about his own tremendous loss—calves drowned, milk cows drowned, dairy barn destroyed, house flooded.

"They've had some field washing, some vegetable crops lost, but nothing like the loss you've experienced. Nothing that even came close," said C.J.

Changing the subject, John asked, "You fought in Afghanistan, right?"

"Yes, I did," said C.J.

"Well, you probably didn't know this, but I spent a couple years in the army as well," said John.

"I did not know that," said C.J.

"It was back in 1990–91. I was a part of the First Gulf War. I was in the First Infantry Division," said John. "Never got a scratch. Lucky I guess."

A knock came on the door, followed by, "It's me." Maggie sounded excited.

"Come in, come in," said C.J.

"Oh, I didn't realize you had company," she said, surprised to see the Wilsons.

"The Wilsons are staying with me until they can get their flooded house back in order," said C.J.

"Thanks for all your help, Maggie," said John. "I don't know what I would have done if all of you vets hadn't shown up. We'd probably have lost more cows than we did."

"I've got news, big news," Maggie said, nearly out of breath.

"You want Florence and me to go outside so you can talk to C.J.?" John asked.

"No, you should hear this too," said Maggie. "Remember my friend at the Pentagon who got an interpretation on the homestead contract that appeared to give the pipeline company permission to lay their pipes through the disabled vets' land? Well, she's found more. Lots more. Remember how the fund was named after Richard

Barnes's son, who was killed in Iraq? Well, guess what? Barnes's son was not killed in the war. Barnes never even had a son!"

"You sure about that? I met with Barnes, and he was almost crying when he talked about his son," said C.J.

"My friend is good at what she does. Very good. She digs deep. Know what else? You'll fall off your chair when I tell you. This guy Barnes is not who he claims to be. Yes, there is a Herman Barnes Family Foundation. But Richard Barnes is also the executive vice president of the Prairie Land Oil Company in Texas. And that's not all." Maggie took a deep breath. "The Prairie Land Oil Company owns the Al-Mid Pipeline Company."

"What?" said C.J., who was having difficulty believing what he was hearing.

"I began connecting the dots," said Maggie. "And here's what I've come up with. Barnes and the Al-Mid Pipeline Company knew from the very beginning that the best route for the pipeline was through Settlers Valley. They researched who owned land in the valley and discovered that disabled veterans had rent-to-buy agreements for land that matched perfectly with where the pipeline company wished to lay its pipes. By offering the veterans money to buy their land using the Josh Barnes Memorial Homestead Fund, they buried a provision in the contract that said by accepting the payment, the company would have access to their land. Thus they could avoid lease payments and all the fuss trying to invoke public domain rules to get permission to build the pipeline. They also hoped to gain some positive publicity."

"Good God," said C.J. "Barnes surely pulled the wool over our eyes. The guy has no morals. He's no more than a crook. Imagine, taking advantage of disabled veterans this way."

"What's next?" asked C.J.

"First, I'll contact each of the vets to let them know what I found. I'm going to the media with the story, which I'm guessing will make national headlines. And then, well, I guess we'll have to see what Barnes does. There is another clause in the contract that says in effect, if the recipient of the homestead grant does not make improvements from one year to the next, they must give back the money they received to buy their land. We'll have to see if Barnes will sue to get his money back," said Maggie.

Listening attentively to Maggie's report, John Wilson said, "This guy from the pipeline company, what was his name, Sage, he was one smooth operator. He offered me a pile of money if I'd sign a lease for the pipeline to stretch across my property. I checked with my attorney, and my attorney said it sounded like a good deal. So I planned to sign on the dotted line. I was supposed to do it today. That Sage fellow and that pipeline company are crooked as snakes. He'll get no signature from me."

"Thank you," said C.J.

"Know what else this Sage guy said? He said without permission to build on my land, the pipeline wouldn't build at all. He said it was just too expensive to build on any of the alternate routes," said John. "He said that's why he was offering me more money than usual for a lease to build on my land."

"Do you suppose he was right about that? If you don't sign a lease, the pipeline project is dead?" asked Maggie.

"I think he meant what he was saying," said John.

# 51

*Ames County Argus*
FLOODING IN SETTLERS VALLEY
DESTROYS WILSON FARM

This past week's rainstorm and flooding in Settlers Valley devastated the John Wilson dairy farm located there. High winds associated with the storm tore off the roof and collapsed one entire sidewall of Wilson's dairy barn that housed some of his large herd of Holstein milk cows. Flood waters drowned 50 calves that were housed in individual calf hutches. The exact number of cows that were either drowned or killed is not known. The surviving cattle have been trucked to the Lazy Z Dairy Farm in nearby Winnebago County.

Mr. Wilson, when asked if he would rebuild, said, "I don't know. I really don't know. I have some insurance, but surely not enough to cover this loss. Florence and I want to thank the Back to the Land Veterans living here in Settlers Valley, who, to a person, came to help us. We are forever grateful for their kindness and their willingness to help move our surviving cattle and help prevent our home from flooding more than it did."

Green Bay television weather forecaster Penny Bright said, "The recent storm, which dumped 15 inches of rain in the valley in 24 hours, was a history maker. There are no weather records to suggest that Settlers Creek, which seldom overflows its banks, has ever caused severe flooding in the valley. This is probably a 500-year weather event."

Meanwhile, the veterans survived the storm remarkably well. C.J. Anderson, spokesperson for the Back to the Land Veterans, said, "We suffered little damage to our various crops and farming enterprises. On the plus side, the valley surely needed the rain as most crops were suffering from the extended drought. I must add that we all felt bad about what happened to John Wilson's farm, and the tremendous loss of dairy animals' lives and the destruction and flooding of his farm buildings."

"You get your feet wet in the flood?" asked Oscar as the two old-timers pulled up chairs at the Eat Well.

"That was something," said Fred. "I can remember a long way back, and I don't remember Settlers Creek floodin' the entire valley. And no I didn't get my feet wet. I spent some money on good boots."

"John Wilson surely got hammered," said Oscar.

"He sure did. You know, Oscar, and I hate to say this, but some-times it takes somethin' like this to bring a community together. Old John was off there by himself, lookin' down on the disabled vets and poo-pooin' their way of farmin'. He really didn't have much to do with the vets. I think he was surprised when he saw them droppin' everythin' and rushin' to his farm to help."

"Fred, you nailed it. I was thinkin' the same thing," said Oscar. "I think Wilson just about dropped his teeth when C.J. invited him and his wife to live with him until they could dry out their flooded house."

"Wonder what he's gonna do?" asked Fred.

"I asked C.J. about that, and C.J. said John had been talkin' to his friend who runs the Lazy Z Dairy Farm in Winnebago County. These guys attended the University of Wisconsin's Farm Short Course together some years ago. His friend at the Lazy Z is takin' care of

John's cows until he decides what to do next. You know what?" said Oscar, who this morning was working on a plate of scrambled eggs and bacon.

"What?" said Fred, who had a pile of pancakes in front of him and was pouring syrup over them.

"This friend of John's, who one time milked more than five hundred cows and kept them confined in a big barn, just as John was doin', sold off all his cows except for eighty-five of the best ones," said Oscar.

"Why'd he do that?" asked Fred, who had commenced working on the pancakes.

"This guy is doin' what's called rotational grazin', which means he has his eighty-five cows outside on pasture durin' all the pasture growin' months of the year. They only come inside to be milked," said Oscar.

"Sounds a lot like how we did it, Oscar, back when we were in the cow milkin' business," said Fred.

"There are some differences. I don't recall that I ever milked more than thirty-five cows and this guy has eighty-five. And he doesn't just turn the cows out to one pasture. With electric fences, he keeps moving the fence every few days so the pasture where they've been can recover, and the new pasture is always fresh and lush."

"So what's that got to do with John Wilson?" asked Fred.

"C.J. told me that Wilson believes that God has talked to him with this storm and flood. And now Wilson is seriously thinkin' of doin' just what his friend is doin'. Parin' his herd down to about eighty-five cows and then puttin' them out on pasture," said Oscar.

"Well, I'll be," said Fred. "I thought Wilson was so caught up with the bigger-is-better approach to farmin' that he'd come back with more cows than he had before," said Fred.

"Aside from some of his strange beliefs, John Wilson is not dumb. He explained to C.J. how the price of milk has been goin' up and down like a roller coaster, and that recently he was essentially milkin' cows for nothin'—his expenses equaled his income. With this rotational grazin' approach, he needs a lot less help, and he doesn't have to worry about a big manure spill, as most of the year the cows are spreadin' their own manure. His friend at the Lazy Z told him that the cows seem a lot happier when they are out in the sunshine, eating grass, and getting lots of exercise," said Oscar.

They both sat quietly for a minute or so, working on their breakfasts.

"I've got some more big news," said Oscar.

"Well, you are just filled with news today," said Fred.

"I just got this from C.J., and you can't tell anybody about it until all the Back to the Land vets hear about it," said Oscar.

"Mum's the word," said Fred as he quit eating in preparation for the news.

"Richard Barnes is a fraud and no friend of the disabled vets," began Oscar.

"Really, I thought you were high on the guy?"

"I was until I heard what I'm about to tell you," said Oscar. "Maggie Werch has a lawyer friend at the Pentagon, and she dug out some interestin' stuff."

Oscar went on to explain how Barnes had made up the story about losing a son in the war. "The guy never even had a son."

"Really?" said Fred, having difficulty believing what he was hearing.

"There's a Herman Barnes Family Foundation, but its purpose in offerin' homestead grants to the veterans was to help the Al-Mid Pipeline Company get permissions for diggin' in their pipeline. And you know what else? The Al-Mid Pipeline Company is owned by the Prairie Land Oil Company in Texas. And guess who is the vice president of the oil company?" asked Oscar.

"Not Richard Barnes, the great friend of disabled vets?"

"One and the same," said Oscar. "That man is a connivin' crook."

"But didn't his foundation invest big bucks so the vets could buy their own land, followin' the idea of the old homestead laws?"

"Yes, they did," answered Oscar. "But the homestead contract the vets signed had a provision in it that essentially gave the pipeline company permission to build without leases or any other kind of permission."

"But the vets still have their land, right?" asked Fred.

"I'm not so sure," said Oscar. "And neither are Maggie and C.J. They aren't convinced the vets will be able to keep their land. There's another provision in the contract that says each person receiving a homestead contract and money must show improvement each year for five years. I'm just guessin', but this scoundrel Barnes will try to get his money back—and he'll have that improvement business as his argument."

"Jeez, these poor vets have one calamity after another," said Fred.

# 52

On a warm, early September day, Joe Berry and a busload of elementary students were harvesting vegetables in the school garden. The heavy rain had done little harm to the school forest and the school garden, as it had done to others living in the valley. The rain allowed Berry to put away the irrigation equipment that had kept the garden alive during the drought. As Berry knew from his farming days, nothing beats rainwater for helping crops grow.

One group of three students was digging carrots. And a student with a wide-tined fork dug the carrots, another student cut off the green tops, and a third tossed the beautiful orange vegetable in bushel baskets. A second group harvested tomatoes, leaving behind the green ones, which would turn red in a few days. They had filled one bushel basket and were working on a second. A third group picked green beans. With the recent rain and now sunny, bright days, the bean plants had flourished. This group already had filled a large pail with green beans.

Joe Berry worked with a fourth group that had volunteered to dig potatoes. He showed them how to use a six-tine fork to dig the potatoes from the ground while avoiding piercing a potato with a tine. He explained to the group that once a potato was stabbed with a fork tine, it would spoil and must be set aside for early eating.

Joe looked up to see the school principal, Lucy James, park her car and walk toward him.

"How's it going?" Lucy asked Joe by way of greeting. Visiting the school forest and its garden was one of her favorite things to do.

"Pretty well. These kids learn quickly, and besides, they seem to be having a good time. The vegetable crop looks pretty good too. Looks better than I thought it would be, given that stretch of dry weather."

"Any of the kids ask about the guy who committed suicide back in the woods where he had been camping?" asked Lucy.

"No, they haven't. Terrible thing that was. To think that this guy was camping right here under our noses and living off the few vegetables he stole from our garden. He was also the one who ran off with my trail camera," said Joe. "To think that this guy, a disabled veteran himself, was responsible for all the terrible things that happened here in the valley this year. I'm told this fellow had PTSD real bad."

"Well, I've got some good news to share," said Lucy. "A biologist from the Department of Natural Resources stopped by my office the other day. He wanted permission to do a bit of exploring in the school forest. He wanted to check out what types of trees grow in our forest, what kinds of birds nest there, and what sort of critters live in the wetlands along the Settlers Creek that twists through the forest."

"What'd he find?"

"It's what he didn't find that was most interesting in the report he gave me."

"Whatta you mean, didn't find?" asked Joe.

"He found the patch of lupines, and he wondered if we'd ever seen a Karner blue butterfly there, especially in late May and early June when the lupines are in full bloom. I showed him some of the photos I'd taken last spring of various kinds of butterflies. Guess what? I had a couple of Karner blue photos."

"Well, that's great. Somethin' special about Karner blue butterflies?" asked Joe.

"Yes, indeed. These little butterflies are on the federal endangered list. The DNR guy said they would all disappear if something should happen to the wild lupines. It seems the Karner blues depend on wild lupines as a food source and a place where they lay their eggs," said Lucy.

"Well, well," said Joe. "I think I know where this conversation is going and might I add the words Al-Mid Pipeline to see if my thinkin' is matchin' yours."

"You are on to it, Joe," Lucy said, smiling. "Our lupine patch and the Karner blue butterfly would prevent the pipeline ever coming through the school forest."

"Did you hear that John Wilson, the farmer who was flooded out in the big rainstorm and lost so many cows and calves, has decided that he won't sign a lease for the pipeline to cross his land, either?" asked Joe. "My old farmer friend shared this bit of news with me. Pipeline guy said that if they couldn't lease land from John Wilson, they'd have to find another route for the pipeline."

"I'm glad we don't have to worry about the pipeline. Wonder what's next? There's always something or somebody who doesn't agree with what we're doing," said Lucy.

"I hope the disabled vets tryin' to farm here in the valley are feeling a little better. They've had a tough time this year. I still can't believe that one of their group caused all the troubles they've had, including the church burnin'. And then that goll darn pipeline wanted to come to our valley. The year's been a bugger," said Joe.

# 53

Richard Barnes, associated with the Herman Barnes Family
Foundation of Texas, has been discovered to also be an executive
with the Prairie Land Oil Company. Prairie Land owns the
Al-Mid Pipeline Company, which has been seeking leases to
cross Settlers Valley, where 20 disabled veterans farm.

Barnes had befriended C.J. Anderson, a leader of the Back to the
Land Veterans group, and claimed he wanted to help the disabled
veterans in the name of his son, who had been killed in Iraq. The
Herman Barnes Family Foundation gave money to the veterans
so they could purchase the property on which they farmed, in a
program somewhat similar to the historic Homestead Act of
1862, which offered thousands of acres of federally owned land
to those wishing to farm it. Each disabled veteran signed a
contract stating that the recipient of the homestead grant money
must (1) live on the land, (2) till the soil and (3) make yearly
improvements. If these provisions were followed for five years,
the farmer was to gain full ownership of the property.

What looked like a generous offer for cash-strapped disabled
veterans was actually a ploy for the Al-Mid Pipeline Company to

automatically gain permission to cross these farms without having to negotiate leases. Buried in the contract was this provision: "Recipients of this homestead grant, within the five years of their probationary time, must allow any person or persons working for the public interest to have access to this land." The pipeline company has long argued that transporting petroleum, natural gas and other such products is in the public interest.

With the plan uncovered, landowners previously open to granting lease permissions have withdrawn their interest, leaving the pipeline company unable to build in their preferred location. Meanwhile, the Herman Barnes Family Foundation attempted to sue each of the disabled veterans, claiming that the farmers had not made sufficient improvements on their land as specified in their contracts and must return the money the foundation gave them to purchase their small-acreage farms.

The Barnes Foundation's attorney presented its case in front of Ames County judge Hector Hennessey. Judge Hennessey, upon reviewing the homestead contract, promptly threw out the case, stating, "How can you argue that these disabled veterans have not made improvements on their land? It's been but six months since these veterans received the so-called homestead money. Under the provisions of the homestead contract, these disabled veterans have five years to show that they have made improvements."

"Oscar, did you read the story in this week's *Argus* about your friend Barnes suin' the disabled vets to get back the money that they awarded them?" said Fred as they ate breakfast at the Eat Well.

"Fred, that bastard is no friend of mine," said Oscar, raising his voice. "I'd like to kick his ass. What a connivin' crook. He pulled one over on me, that's for damn sure. Can you imagine the gall of a guy to come up with a story about a son killed in the war? The guy's got guts, I'll give him that. He ought to be in jail. That's where he outta be."

"You got that right," said Fred.

"Maggie is really pissed off at how this guy tried to come off as a sympathetic friend of disabled veterans and all he wanted was for his damn pipeline to stretch through our valley. She's puttin' this story up on the social media—that internet stuff that she knows about and I scarcely know how to talk about. She wants to make sure no other veteran group will be taken in like they were," said Oscar.

"From what I understand about the judge's decision, the veterans get to keep their farms, as long as they follow the provisions of their contracts. If they do what the contract says, in five years the land is theirs," said Fred.

"That's right, unless another 'in the public interest' outfit comes along," said Oscar.

"These vets have gone through enough this year. Pastor Vicki told me she sees progress. The idea of the land healin' a person seems to be workin'. It would be just awful for them to lose their land just as they are makin' good progress," said Fred.

"Well, maybe we are on the verge of seein' a little 'normal' return to Settlers Valley. It's almost time to help the newcomer veterans learn how to put their farms to bed for the winter. I'll bet doughnuts to dollars that the newest ones don't know how to do it," said Oscar.

"Aren't you the know-it-all," said Fred.

"All I'm doing is offerin' a little help. I suspect you may get into the act as well. I'll bet the vets growin' vegetables don't know about cover crops and how important they are both to keep their sandy land from blowin' away and providin' another source of organic material for their soil."

"Been meanin' to ask," began Fred, changing the subject. "How's that scribblin' class you're teachin' workin' out?"

"Fred, it is not a scribblin' class. It's known as the Red Barn Writers' Workshop," said Oscar.

"Kind of a fancy title for a bunch of novice writers," said Fred.

"Well, the name may sound fancy to you, Fred, but to this group of vets it's surely not. By the way, Fred, when is the last time you wrote more than a sentence?"

"Oscar, I'm proud to say that I am a looker and a reader and not a writer."

"The veterans in this workshop are doing one outstandin' job," said Oscar, proudly.

"Good to hear," said Fred, who was munching on a piece of toast smeared with butter and a thick layer of strawberry jam.

"A couple of the vets have written stories about their war experiences and have had them published in a national veteran's newsletter. Maggie is writing a book about what's going on here in Settlers Valley, and the group is publishing *The Disabled Veterans of Settlers Valley*, a collection of stories that they have written," said Oscar.

"Well, good for them," said Fred. "I just might have to break my rule about not readin' books."

# 54

October in central Wisconsin should be awarded the prize for the most strikingly beautiful month of the year. In Link Lake and nearby Settlers Valley, maples show off their reds and yellows, aspens their deep yellow, oaks their several shades of brown and tan. Sumac, one of the early starters of the color parade, shows its presence with its brilliant reds, as does the Virginia creeper that crawls to the top of many of the trees in the valley.

October in central Wisconsin is a time for celebration. It is the month when harvesting is complete, the field crops are in, the hay is stored, and the last vegetable crops—the late potatoes, late sweet corn, and the squash and pumpkins—are harvested and stored. With the fall work completed, farmers in the valley relax a bit and make ready for the long winter ahead. And they celebrate.

Construction of the new Link Lake People's Church was completed. No longer do churchgoers gather in the former hayloft of Oscar Anderson's barn, although several of the regular churchgoers had commented that there was something natural about worshipping in a barn. On this mid-October Saturday afternoon, Pastor Vicki was looking forward to a special celebration at the new church: a wedding.

Pastor Vicki looked out the window of the little office that was a part of her living quarters in the back of the church. The sky was the deepest blue she ever remembered. She glanced at the thermometer, which read sixty degrees. It would be a great day for a wedding. She thought back to when she arrived at Link Lake in response to an article she had read in *Reader's Digest*. She knew all too well the agony many disabled vets faced after they left the military. She had wanted to help, not only by providing a place where the veterans could have a spiritual home but by visiting them on their farms, listening to them share their troubled pasts and their present-day challenges. She felt good about how much progress these vets had made in overcoming, and in many cases learning to live with, their various disabilities. But she couldn't get out of her mind what she considered her most dramatic failure. *I failed Randy Budwell, failed him utterly, maybe even contributed to his mental illness*, thought Vicki. *What could I have done differently? Why didn't I act on the signs that I saw? He was an alcoholic. Unlike the other disabled vets, he absolutely hated farming. Somehow I believed that the veterans hospital might help him, even cure him. Why didn't I follow up with the hospital? If I had, I would have learned about his leaving the hospital, and maybe none of what he did in his deranged mental state would have happened, including burning our church. Perhaps he would still be alive.*

As a trained counselor, Pastor Vicki knew she must quit beating up on herself and move on. "You can't win them all," one of her college instructors had said. At the time the words seemed practical. But failing is not easy to reckon with, especially when you think it might make a difference if a person lives or dies.

Pastor Vicki knew she must get over her funk before the afternoon wedding ceremony. She thought about what she considered her most significant achievement—sitting down over a cup of coffee with the Reverend Jacob John Jacob. Their first meeting at the Eat Well was a bit frosty. By an unspoken agreement, they had avoided arguing over their theological differences. They soon discovered they had several things in common, most notably their commitment to being of service to the more extensive Link Lake community. The reverend and Pastor Vicki had continued to meet for coffee every two weeks, and although they clearly differed on many matters, they discovered that they liked each other, much to the surprise of each of them.

It was time to prepare the church for the afternoon ceremony. Several veterans and their spouses arrived by late morning to do a bit of decorating in the church. Pastor Vicki also met with the committee of veterans that was planning the reception and wedding dance to be held at Oscar Anderson's barn loft, a place that had become a second home for several of the vets.

By two thirty, the church was nearly filled. Pastor Vicki, glancing around the group, was quite sure every one of the disabled vets and their spouses and children was in attendance. She also saw several of the businesspeople in Link Lake and their spouses, and several people she did not recognize. Of course, Fred Russo was there, and sitting with him were John Wilson and his wife. Before the flood, Wilson had nothing to do with either Fred or Oscar. *How things can change*, thought Vicki.

Promptly at three o' clock, the church's new pianist began playing "I Can't Help Falling in Love" as Pastor Vicki, C.J. Anderson, and C.J.'s grandpa Oscar entered and stood to face the congregation. Both Andersons wore suits and neckties, and each had a single red rose pinned to his lapel. Next to enter was Lucy James, wearing a simple tan dress and carrying a bouquet of roses. She took her place to the right of Pastor Vicki. Everyone now stood, as the organist began playing "Here Comes the Bride." Maggie Werch, wearing a simple white wedding gown and carrying a bouquet of red roses, slowly walked from the back of the church on the arm of her father, who had come with Maggie's mother from Chicago to the wedding ceremony. Maggie's father, a short, thin man, arrived at the front of the church. He left Maggie at the altar and took his seat next to Maggie's mother in the first row.

Pastor Vicki began, "We are gathered here today to witness the joining of these two lives. C.J. and Maggie met here in the valley, fell in love, and are finalizing their love with this marriage. Now, a few words from C.J.'s grandfather Oscar Anderson."

Oscar walked to the lectern, took a piece of paper from his pocket, unfolded it, and began reading.

*To Maggie and C.J.*
On this October day,
We celebrate the marriage of Maggie and C.J.
Farmers in this valley we call Settlers.
Back to the Land farmers, we call them.
Looking to heal the land.
As the land heals them.
Combining their talents and love,
For each other and for the land.
For today, and for tomorrow, and,
As our Native American friends state so eloquently,
For seven generations into the future.
My buttons are bursting with pride.
For these young people in what they have accomplished.
And for what they yet will accomplish
As they till the soil
And nurture their love for each other.
Godspeed to both of you.

Oscar returned to stand next to his grandson. C.J. and Maggie now moved to stand facing each other and holding hands. Pastor Vicki, looking at C.J., said, "C.J., do you take Maggie to be your wife? Do you promise to love, honor, cherish, and protect her in good times and bad, in sickness and in health, until death do you part? If so, answer with, 'I do.'"

"I do," said C.J., smiling.

Turning to Maggie, Pastor Vicki said, "Maggie, do you take C.J. to be your husband? Do you promise to love, honor, cherish, and protect him in good times and bad, in sickness and in health, until death do you part? If so, answer with, 'I do.'"

"I do," said Maggie in a loud, clear voice.

After the exchanging of rings, Pastor Vicki said, "I now pronounce you husband and wife. You may kiss the bride," which C.J. promptly did. Then they walked down the aisle hand in hand to clapping and cheers.

From the church, everyone drove out to Oscar Anderson's farm, where the hayloft of his old red barn had been decorated in red, white, and blue to commemorate the military service of C.J. and Maggie. The Link Lake Brewery provided free Settlers Brew, made from veteran-grown barley and hops, as well as root beer. Ben Rostum had donated free-range chickens. Shortly after people began arriving, they could smell the broilers on Ben's big charcoal grill. Several big bowls of vegetable salad stood on the banquet table, along with tubs of homemade sauerkraut and trays of dill pickles, sweet and sour pickles, and pickled beets, all homegrown on disabled veterans' farms and donated for the celebration.

As people lined up to fill their plates, Lucy James played background music on the keyboard. C.J. and Maggie walked from table to table, greeting people and thanking those who had donated food. After everyone had gone through the food line, C.J. and Maggie cut the big wedding cake that one of the veterans had baked. Following a long-standing tradition, Maggie fed the first piece of cake to C.J.

A little before six, the Settler Valley Ramblers, minus their trumpet player, began tuning up, and promptly at six, the Ramblers started playing the "Tennessee Waltz." C.J. was not the greatest dancer, but he and Maggie led off, both smiling and Maggie trying to avoid having her feet stomped on by her new husband's big feet.

Dancing, eating, and drinking continued into the warm October evening, as a big yellow harvest moon appeared on the horizon. By the time the celebration was coming to an end, the moon hung over the old red barn, a symbol, someone had said, of better days ahead for the Back to the Land Veterans, their friends in Settlers Valley, and the Link Lake community.

# Acknowledgments

As is the case for all my work, a number of people helped me along the way. My wife, Ruth, as first reader, passes judgment on every word I write. If what I write doesn't make it past Ruth, it goes nowhere.

My daughter, Sue, a published author, and my daughter-in-law, Natasha, a professional journalist, read early drafts of the manuscript and offered many useful suggestions for both character and plot development.

My son Steve, a professional photographer with a journalism degree, is a big-picture critic of my work, and my son Jeff, a Colorado businessperson, offered practical suggestions for making the story both interesting as well as plausible.

My grandson Josh Horman, a third-year law student, served as my consultant for the scenes where I wrote about laws.

My cousin Dennis Apps, a retired police detective from the Milwaukee police department, helped with the scenes that involved police procedure.

A huge thank you to Colonel Donavan Klimpel, U.S. Army retired, who read the entire manuscript and helped me make sure that what I was writing about disabled veterans was authentic.

I can never thank Kate Thompson, freelance editor, enough. She has an uncanny way of taking my sometimes-tangled writing and making it readable. She has worked on each of my novels over the years.

Thanks also to Sheila McMahon, senior project editor, for overseeing the editorial process for this novel, and Michelle Wing, who did a super job of copyediting.

Lastly, I want to thank Dennis Lloyd, director of the University of Wisconsin Press, who saw this book through its approval process and supported its publication.

## BOOKS BY JERRY APPS

FICTION

*The Travels of Increase Joseph*
*In a Pickle: A Family Farm Story*
*Blue Shadows Farm*
*Cranberry Red*
*Tamarack River Ghost*
*The Great Sand Fracas of Ames County*
*Cold as Thunder*
*Settlers Valley*

NONFICTION

*Problems in Continuing Education*
*Improving Practice in Continuing Education*
*Higher Education in a Learning Society*
*Mastering the Teaching of Adults*
*Teaching from the Heart*
*Leadership for the Emerging Age*
*Telling Your Story*
*The Land Still Lives*
*Barns of Wisconsin*
*Mills of Wisconsin*
*Humor from the Country*
*Breweries of Wisconsin*
*One-Room Country Schools*
*Rural Wisdom*
*Cheese: The Making of a Wisconsin Tradition*

When Chores Were Done
Ringlingville USA
Every Farm Tells a Story
Country Ways and Country Days
Living a Country Year
Old Farm: A History
Horse-Drawn Days: A Century of Farming with Horses
Garden Wisdom: Lessons Learned From 60 Years of Gardening
The Quiet Season
Limping Through Life: A Farm Boy's Polio Memoir
Whispers and Shadows
The People Came First: The History of Wisconsin Cooperative
    Extension
Wisconsin Agriculture: A History
Roshara Journal: Four Seasons, Fifty Years and 120 Acres
Campfires and Loon Calls
Never Curse the Rain
Old Farm Country Cookbook
Once a Professor
Cheese: The Making of a Wisconsin Tradition, 2nd ed.
The Old Timer Says
When the White Pine Was King
The Civilian Conservation Corps in Wisconsin

CHILDREN AND YOUNG ADULT BOOKS
Stormy
Eat Rutabagas
Letters from Hillside Farm (fiction)
Casper Jaggi: Master Cheese Maker
Tents, Tigers and the Ringling Brothers